Under a Klondike Sky

Ava Wilson

Under a Klondike Sky

AVA C. WILSON

CROOKED RIVER PUBLISHING
Terrebonne, Oregon

To order, visit our website www.avawilsonauthor.com

Printed in the United States of America at Gorham Printing, Centralia, WA

ISBN 978-0-615-63536-1

Dedicated to our amazing daughters, Danise, Kim, and Joanna, my own heroines.

I

. . . .

DIRECTIONS TO THE HOUSE SPECIFICALLY SAID TO turn right at the gas station and follow the road one mile to a driveway on the left. Rosalie mumbled to herself that her idea of a driveway was fifty feet of concrete leading to a two car garage; instead, this was merely a desert track with stiff weeds scraping the undercarriage of her car. Hardened ruts showed evidence of muddy pitfalls during wetter seasons. Rosalie could see the aged two-story ranch house looming about a half-mile away.

Nearer the house, she was met by a huge yellow dog that resembled a lab, but barked like a hound. He ran around and around her car as she crept along the track, barking joyously as if they were already friends. When Rosalie stopped, the dust that had been following in her wake enveloped the car in a gritty cloud; keeping the door shut and windows up for a couple of minutes seemed a good idea.

Precisely at the moment Rosalie shut off the car's engine, a thin, white-haired woman stepped from behind a screen door.

"The lawyer said you'd be on time, and here you are," she said, taking her hands out of her Mother Hubbard apron pockets. "Buddy, quiet!" she admonished, and the dog, grinning widely, wriggled to her side. The stained apron covered a red checkered shirt and denim pants, and Rosalie noticed the elderly woman was wearing scuffed Wellingtons.

"And you must be Mrs. Granger," Rosalie said, offering her hand in greeting. She followed the rancher into an old-fashioned parlor, complete with an antique piano and swivel stool. The Portland lawyer had explained to Rosalie that an antiques dealer was scheduled to arrange a barn sale next month, but she was not experienced in valuing old books. As owner of Driftwood Books, a used bookstore in Portland, Oregon, Rosalie had been recommended as being fair in her offers to purchase book collections. Always excited about examining books in obscure locations, she didn't even mind the three-hour drive to the high desert of central Oregon.

"This is my first visit to Shaniko; have you always lived here, Mrs. Granger?" asked Rosalie.

"Well, first off, call me Callie. My husband and I grew up in Antelope, just a few miles south of here. This old place was built by my Grandpa Storey about 1900, when sheep ranching was big in these parts. Back then, you know, this area was still called Cross Hollows. When Grandpa passed away, Uncle Bill took over and since he never married or had children, I inherited the ranch. We had been ranching near Prineville, but jumped at the chance to get back to these hills."

"If you don't mind my asking, when did your ancestors come west? Were they part of the Oregon Trail pioneers?" Rosalie asked.

"Dad's family came out in 1849 from back east and settled in the Willamette Valley first. Later they scattered and some took up land on this side of the Cascade Mountains because they thought it was getting too crowded over there," Callie answered.

"It is certainly beautiful out here, very different from over on the west side of the Cascades," Rosalie said, as she scanned the autumn landscape.

"You get too much rain over there," Callie replied, in a way that left no doubt which was the best place to live.

Callie led Rosalie up a narrow staircase to a room unmistakably used as a woman's sewing and reading retreat. An old Singer sewing machine stood ready to make an apron with the gingham material folded on the stool, and a cutting table took up the center of the room. Across the room, a chintz-covered chaise lounge reclined by the westward facing window. Pointing to the wall at the far end of the room, Callie said, "I realize that most of these are just old books, but some might mean something to someone. I'd like for you to take them all, and give me a fair offer for the lot. Some are near a hundred years old, bought by my grandma and Mother. I've read just about all of them, and added some of my own through the years. Our daughter lives in Seattle, and already has what she wants of the books and mementos from the ranch." Then, leaning forward, she confided, "She's a citified girl."

Rosalie couldn't decide if Callie was proud of that fact, or just explaining why her daughter didn't want any more of the vintage furnishings.

"We gave a few things to some friends and relatives, but plan to sell what's in the barn and a few household furnishings. I guess they're collectible, being old." She leaned on a corner of the cutting table. "We lost our only son in Vietnam, so we're selling the ranchland to a good neighbor who has land joining ours. This old house and a few acres are being deeded to the county historical society. We'll leave most of this furniture to display for the public. I've got a little house in Redmond, close to the nursing home where Lem is… I don't get back out here much." The old rancher looked around, "I sure loved this room, spent many an afternoon up here."

Rosalie nodded, and realized Callie just needed to talk to someone, even a stranger.

Callie added, "Anything we make from selling our belongings will go to charities; we like that idea."

"What a wonderful legacy from such a historic place as this." Rosalie assured her.

"I sure miss the old days out here," she added wistfully.

Rosalie felt a genuine sadness for Callie Granger; most likely the old couple had envisioned a different life in their later years. She turned to survey the book shelves, remarking on specific titles.

Callie finally said, "Well, I've got a few things to do in the barn, so make yourself at home while looking at the books. I guess you'll need awhile to see if they are worth anything much."

"If you can give me about an hour, I'll have an offer for you," Rosalie gently replied as Callie left the room. Over her shoulder the old woman added, "I'll start the electric percolator, so get some coffee when it smells done."

Rosalie set her bag on the chaise lounge and imagined how women through the last century might have reclined there, reading in the afternoons. She pictured a pompadour coiffed woman, perhaps attired in a long skirt and puffy-sleeved blouse; another in a plain cotton house dress with sturdy shoes, and stockings rolled down to her ankles. "Better get busy!" Rosalie said out loud.

Through many years of practice, Rosalie could examine hundreds of books in a short time, and pick out the ones that were rare or collectible. The rest would make acceptable general stock in various sections of Driftwood Books. Rosalie moved the step stool closer to reach the top shelves, and began transferring books to the table, sorting as she went. On one end she placed the collectible books; on the other, books for general stock. Callie Granger's collection included fiction and non-fiction, some children's classics, and books with beautifully illustrated covers from the early 1900's. In just a few minutes, Rosalie had separated from the collection a copy of Tennyson's *Lady of the Lake*, illustrated by Howard Chandler Christy and early editions of Robert Service's *Ballads of a Cheechako*, and *Spell of the Yukon*. She also found several non-fiction titles, including a dozen about Alaska, mostly regarding gold rush days.

As Rosalie worked her way down the shelves, she had to move an old round sewing basket that was supported by three scrolled legs. Knowing a little about antiques, Rosalie believed it was close to one hundred years old.

Turning her attention to a shelf containing old references on ranching and animal husbandry, she soon completed her appraisal of Callie Granger's collection. Precisely one hour after Callie had left the house, she appeared at the sewing room's door.

"I brought you a cup of coffee, seeing that you didn't take the time to go downstairs. Hope you like it black. How're you comin' along?"

"Black is great, thanks. Let me show you some of the best books, the ones I can sell as collectible or rare," Rosalie answered, taking the mug from her. Callie Granger exclaimed, "Lordy!" when she pointed out the values of a Steinbeck first edition and three books by Frank Baum which included *The Wonderful Wizard of Oz*. The most amazing find was a first edition of *Gone with the Wind*, complete with a slightly frayed dust wrapper, which would retail for $2200. After Callie recovered from the shock of such treasures on the sewing room shelves, she decided to keep *Smokey, the Cow Horse* by Will James, for her neighbor's grandson, and Theodore Roosevelt's *Ranch Life and the Hunting-Trail*, for a nephew in Wyoming. Callie assured Rosalie she had already set aside a few books to keep for herself; however, she removed from the table a leather-bound copy of *Cattle of the World*. Getting down to business, Rosalie quoted her best offer for the collection, adding that it was one of the best she had seen in a private home; Callie was candidly pleased, so both of them were happy with the transaction. Rosalie explained that since some of the rarer items would sell quite fast to her serious collectors, she could pay half of their values. The other books would stay on her shelves longer, so she could pay up to twenty-five percent for those.

"I like the idea of these books going to folks who can really appreciate them. You've helped me understand how special some of them are." Callie remarked. Rosalie wrote out the check and smiled to herself when Callie patted the apron pocket where she tucked it.

"I noticed there are several books about Alaska and the Yukon during the gold rush period in your collection. I'm wondering if you know the significance of these particular books." Rosalie asked.

"My Grandma Abigail went to Dawson City in 1898 to marry her fiancé who was a pastor. In fact my momma, Faith, was born up there in the spring of 1899," Callie proudly announced.

"That's amazing! Did your Grandmother tell you much about it?"

"Oh, yes! And she wrote letters from the Klondike to her best friend, Alice, which told so much about her life in that remote place. Alice saved those letters to give to me before she died in 1950. Later I helped Grandma Abigail write a memoir about her years in the North," Callie explained.

"You are so lucky to have such a great family record!" Rosalie said.

"Yes, I know," Callie hesitated, and then added, "I've shared the letters with my daughter, but not the memoir; I guess I should do that soon." Responding to Rosalie's puzzled expression, Callie added, "There are some secrets I've kept from her; I'm not sure how she would take it!"

Rosalie understood, but assured her that many people have a family tree with surprises. Callie laughed, and said, "I suppose you're right."

The two of them went to Rosalie's car for the plastic totes she always carried to estate sales and auctions. Old Buddy, stretched out in the shade of the barn, raised his head to see what they were doing. Satisfied the women weren't going anywhere exciting, he plopped his head back onto the dirt with a bored groan. The lady rancher pointed off toward the rolling hills west of the ranch, which eventually sloped off into the Deschutes River canyon. Sparse vegetation decorated the vista, with occasional ranch houses glimpsed in the valleys. On her drive to Shaniko through the vacant ranchlands, Rosalie had noticed unusual groupings of old cottonwood trees formed in squares, or perfectly straight lines from an unused gate or along an overgrown side road, which she identified as former home sites. Not everyone was successful on their piece of land.

"Over there the last big Indian fight happened over a hundred years ago. It was before this ranch was built, but my grandma used to tell stories her pa had told," Callie informed her.

Rosalie admitted that she knew very little of the history in this part of Oregon. Callie recommended a few books for her to read, two she had just purchased. They carefully packed five totes and used the little folding hand cart to get them to the car. The two women exchanged phone numbers, in case any questions about the collection arose.

"I wish I could get back over here for your barn sale," Rosalie commented, as she searched her bottomless canvas bag for keys. "You folks have some wonderful things that any collector would love to have."

"Is there something in particular you liked?" Callie asked.

"Oh … well … I noticed the tall sewing basket upstairs. I have my own grandmother's treadle sewing machine and I can just imagine how great they would look together in my guest bedroom," Rosalie answered, hopeful that Callie hadn't intended to keep it and she could buy it today.

Callie grinned, saying, "I like the idea of it going home with you; it belonged to my Grandma Storey. Now, I don't want you to try to pay for it."

Protesting, Rosalie shook her head, but the rancher insisted, "I really appreciate the way you dealt with me on the books, being honest about their values. I've made enough money off you today!" They both laughed. Soon, the sewing basket was wedged into the car's front seat.

As she drove back toward the paved road, the yellow dog and the dust followed her down the dirt track. Rosalie saw Callie Granger in her rear view mirror, waving and calling to Buddy. She rather enjoyed the drive home through the Columbia River Gorge, with its quaint historic towns and gorgeous scenery. With the Bee Gees in Concert keeping her company, two hours later Rosalie pulled into her short, concrete driveway in Portland. Her husband, Ray, stepped out the kitchen door, and reported, "Penny came by the shop and offered to close up so I could help you unload the car when you got home. Timing is perfect!" Usually on Wednesdays, Ray volunteered at their grandsons' elementary school; however, today he ran Driftwood Books for Rosalie. After unloading the books onto shelves in their office, and the sewing basket in the guest room, Ray suggested they walk to Mimi's Café for a Bar-B-Que plate. Over dinner Rosalie shared her day, describing the ranch and Callie Granger. The Klondike connection made for a lively discussion, since Ray had read several books on the history of Alaska and the Yukon.

Wiping sauce from her chin, Rosalie said, "She was so nice to give me the sewing basket. I tried to take the lid off, but it's stuck too tight; one more thing for your 'honey-do' list." Ray nodded, but was too interested in sopping up drippings with a slice of white bread, to remember.

It was six months before the lid came off, helped by Rosalie's youngest grandson romping through the house. When the sewing basket toppled over and hit the floor, off popped the lid; instead of spools of thread, several yellowed envelopes shuffled onto the carpet like a deck of cards. The envelopes were addressed to "Mrs. Russell Storey;" Rosalie peeked inside one and when she read "Dear Alice" on the letter, she recalled that Callie's grandmother had written to her friend Alice. She immediately began trying to contact Callie. Getting no answer to her calls, Rosalie did a search on the internet and discovered that Lemmuel Granger passed away two months earlier. Assuming that Callie must be visiting her daughter, Rosalie eventually reached her at home two weeks later.

Rosalie expressed her sympathy about the loss of Lem, but Callie responded that he "wasn't himself" so it was for the best; however, her voice betrayed her bravado. When Callie heard about the sewing basket's contents, she wasn't surprised.

"Oh, I forgot I had stored those letters in there!" she laughed. "Grandma Abigail lived until 1960, and we spent many Sunday afternoons talking about her life. In the letters to Alice, she left out a lot of details, but later she told me everything she could remember."

Rosalie offered to deliver the bundle personally, since she and Ray had been looking for an excuse to spend a few days exploring Central Oregon. They agreed on the next weekend when Penny could run the book store while they were gone. Callie surprised Rosalie by saying if they were interested in hearing about her family history, she would tell them some stories. When Rosalie confirmed they would be honored to hear about her family, Callie suggested they go ahead and read the letter with the oldest date; she would share the rest of what they found in more detail on the weekend. Rosalie wondered if Callie wanted to see their reactions to the stories, before talking to her daughter.

"Some of my ancestors lived unconventional lives. Maybe that's why I'm so ornery!" the old rancher chuckled.

Later that evening, after dinner dishes were loaded into the dishwasher and Rosalie was comfortably settled in her recliner, Ray asked, "Well, what are you waiting for? Get that first letter out of the envelope. Aren't you anxious to read it?"

"I thought you'd never ask!" Rosalie laughed.

I I

. . . .

June 2, 1898
Prineville, Oregon

Dear Alice,

You will think I have gone mad, and perhaps it is true. I am leaving home, and I know you will understand my reasons; however you may not agree with the direction I am traveling. Barrett has asked me to join him in Dawson City as his wife. I will leave Prineville tomorrow, by stagecoach to The Dalles, where my journey continues by rail to Seattle. Barrett has made all the arrangements for my passage on a steamship to the Arctic, up the Yukon River through Alaska to the Klondike gold fields. Barrett wrote such an endearing letter describing his church in Dawson City, and he convinced me that my teaching experience would be a great compliment to his work. I don't believe I am in love with him and I am not sure he loves me in the way I always dreamed; nevertheless, I am going. I have no way to leave home unless I marry, and I must get away. One late night this winter Mother came into my room, and said she was praying that Barrett would ask me to marry him. My step-father has become quite violent at times and Mother is afraid that he will eventually hurt one of us. Mother puts herself between Jim and us, trying to placate him, and I worry so much about her. I've tried to save my small teacher's salary, to eventually escape the ranch, but Jim takes it. I felt as if I were destined to a life of hard work on the ranch, and teaching ranchers' children for no personal gain. Jim will not deviate from his narrow opinion of women, and bellows at Mother for her supposed shortcomings. You must remember his temper when you and I would return home after prayer meeting Wednesday evenings. I always wanted you to let me out of the buggy at the gate, to prevent your hearing his drunken rants. One evening this spring he caught me in the barn and wrestled me down in a stall before I scratched his eyes and managed to get away. At that moment I knew had to somehow leave the ranch!

Mother assumed that Barrett would come back from the Yukon, so we could marry and settle in Oregon City, his hometown; however, his plans for the immediate future are to save souls among the gold miners and Indians in the north. Alice, is it wrong for me to agree to such a journey and marriage, when I am not in love with Barrett? Not yet, anyway. I do admire him, and perhaps that has to come first. He believes we will make a handsome couple; his letter was signed, "Affectionately, Barrett." Anyway, we will marry as soon as my boat docks in Dawson City. From what he described in this last letter, there are few reputable white women in the Klondike. Only a small number of men take their wives with them, because the way of thinking is to get the gold quickly, and get back home. I have read in the newspapers about hundreds of women who swarm into the Klondike, to entertain in the saloons and theaters. There are a few families operating businesses or are involved in government affairs in Dawson City, so surely we will have a close association with those citizens, as well as the members of our congregation.

Remember when we met Barrett at the revival held by the Congregational Church? You agreed that he is a handsome man indeed, with his dark red hair and impeccable manners! I now know that he is ten years older than I, and his family is quite well off as owners of a barge company along the Willamette River near Portland. I am sorry that you are not here to see me off; however, being on your honeymoon is a good excuse. By the time you return, I understand that your new ranch house will be ready to occupy near Cross Hollows. I will leave this letter at the hotel there when the stage makes a stop, with instructions to make sure you receive it. Surely Barrett and I will not stay in Dawson City more than a year. Perhaps one day, we will arrive at your front door, surprising you and Russ with a visit. In the meantime, I will write as often as possible about my great adventure.

Barrett's letter instructed me to make arrangements to arrive in Seattle in a month's time, so I spoke with Mr. Carpenter at the Cattlemen's Hotel who said the stage from Prineville, through Ashwood, Cross Hollows and Bakeoven, can get me to The Dalles to catch the Columbia River Railway; with a connection in Portland, I will be in Seattle three days after leaving The Dalles. I have allowed extra time for the journey from Prineville, which should give me three or four days before the ship sails, to purchase a list of items Barrett says I will need. Mother nervously tried to talk to me about what married couples do in bed, but I put her out of her misery by telling her I already knew (well, not everything.) I will trust Barrett with those details. Only two weeks ago Mother and I frantically started sewing petticoats, camisoles, under drawers, skirts and shirtwaists for my trousseau. Emily was a dear, helping corral the boys all day so Mother and I had more time to sew. I will miss my little sister as much as Mother! Jim was sullen because he was losing a ranch hand and a source of income. Any smugness I felt inside was kept hidden from him to prevent retaliation. Mother demanded that he let me spend my last wages on preparations for the trip. I heard them arguing one night; Mother told him she would tell her friends, who would tell their husbands, if he refused the money. The next morning Mother had a bruise on her cheek, but the money was in my top bureau drawer. I wish I could take her, Emily and the boys with me.

Wish me luck!

Your friend, Abigail

"What a treasure," Rosalie said to Ray. "Why don't we have something like this left behind by one of our ancestors?"

"You know more than I do about where you come from. All I know is that I was adopted," Ray replied.

"I guess I do. At least Mom left a few hints about her childhood. I wonder what family tales Callie is hesitant to tell her daughter," Rosalie asked no one in particular.

"I don't know, but it's a good thing the book shop is closed on Mondays. I suspect we'll need an extra day over there," Ray laughed.

I I I

· ·

CALLIE WAS BENT OVER HER FLOWER BEDS, DRESSED comfortably in a long denim skirt and untucked blouse, when they parked at the street's curb in front of the tidy bungalow in Redmond. She greeted Ray as if they were long time friends … Ray had that effect on people. Oversized turkey and avocado sandwiches were already prepared, which were washed down with chilled raspberry tea. Callie informed them that the transfer of her ranch house to the Historical Society was almost complete. She was terribly proud of her heritage, and anxious to share what she had and what she knew. Callie admitted that it had been several years since she had read through the letters and memoir. When she was satisfied that Rosalie and Ray were comfortably seated, she unfolded the next letter written by Abigail.

June 7, 1898
The Dalles, Oregon

Dear Alice,

The Dalles is much larger and busier than I had expected, with freighters on the roads and barges on the wide Columbia River. My train has been delayed, but it's supposed to get back on schedule early tomorrow morning. The trip from Prineville was a wonderful adventure, and I will attempt to tell you about it.

The whole family took me into town, but Jim disappeared into the hotel bar. Mother nervously paced and the boys ran off to the livery. Emily hugged me close and begged me to write often. Mother dabbed at the tears on her cheeks after we clung to each other before I boarded. When the stage pulled away from the hotel and rounded the corner of the next block, I saw her figure being buffeted by the wind, hanky waving wildly at me. I suddenly felt very sad and alone, knowing it would be at least a year before I saw them again. Tears started to dribble from my eyes, and I quickly blotted them away.

When the stage left Prineville, six of us were riding inside and two men topside with the driver. Our ride was terribly uncomfortable for the first few miles since the landscape is dotted with volcanic rocks of all sizes. Some efforts were made to remove or dodge the larger ones; however a schedule must be maintained so our driver seldom slowed. A thunderstorm the previous night had swept through the canyons and foothills; when the rocky roads smoothed out, we fought gummy ruts all the way to Crowder's Station, with mud halfway up the wheels in some stretches. Several times the driver ordered all eight passengers out, in order for the team of horses to get past the bogs. Sometimes the men would have to push on the wheels to help the team. Of course, we women passengers ended up with muddy shoes and dress hems. Back on the stage, once the mud had dried on clothes and boots, the floor of our conveyance looked much like a bare dirt yard. My seat mate was a Mrs. Carnahan who was taking her son to a doctor in The Dalles, seeking help for his seizures. The poor little thing sat like a frightened kitten, fearing the next spell. The child's mother confided to me the father had abandoned them during the winter; looking at her was painfully sad, and she nervously explained that she didn't know what she would do if the new doctor couldn't help her son. Mrs. Carnahan suspected her husband had been struck with gold fever, was in the Klondike, and she didn't expect he would ever come back to them. Her son asked several times a day if his father would be at the big city where they were going. She would always gently reply that she was not sure.

Mrs. Carnahan and I had the benefit of ample space on our bench seat, since her son, Lester, was so small. Across from us sat three rather beefy men, whose elbows overlapped each other. Finally at a stop for the horses to drink from a stream, one of the men retrieved a saddle blanket from the baggage compartment in the back, spread it on the floor, and rested there for awhile, giving his seat mates more room. While the teams were being switched just past the steep grade at Grizzly Mountain, Mrs. Carnahan, Lester, and I took advantage of the necessary out back, washed up, and ate ham sandwiches that Mother had thoughtfully packed early that morning. One of the men riding topside, sort of leered at me as he helped us board the stage. I pretended not to have noticed; however the driver saw it, and scowled at him. The road was a bit better while crossing the bunch grass prairie. All of the passengers seemed revived; however, I suspect one or two of the men had taken some liquid refreshment supplied by the station agent.

Watching the landscape from my open window, I saw that for a long distance the prairie was covered with bitterbrush, their yellow blossoms surely attracting bees in large numbers. When the stage stopped in a draw to rest the horses, I could smell a fragrance reminiscent of the sweetbriar rose. Suddenly, Lester fell to the ground, arching his back, with spittle dribbling from the corners of his mouth. The seizure lasted but two or three minutes, and when he revived, Lester buried his face in his mother's skirt; at six years of age, he was already embarrassed about his condition. We remained there for a few more minutes, and when it was time to board, our stage driver asked if Lester would like to ride top side for a mile or two. The little boy brightened right up, and gave his mother a pleading look, whereupon she agreed, casting an appreciative look at the thoughtful man. The driver kept the team at a slow pace, and when it was time for Lester to come down, he announced that he would grow up to be a stage driver. Mrs. Carnahan hugged him close to her on our seat, and soon he was dozing peacefully. I'll not soon forget that stage driver's kindness.

We made a brief stop in Ashwood, which was bustling with miners. One of the passengers quickly unloaded his belongings; the stage made quick time to Antelope, where the other men disembarked. When we pulled into Cross Hollows for fresh horses, the driver told us the town was going to be moved out of the canyon a short distance, and renamed "Shaniko." It seems that the Indians mispronounced an early German settler's name, and the town organizers decided to use it. I wish I had known where your new home was being built there. The land is so vast, with sweeping views of mountains and plains; really quite beautiful, but of course you already know that. I hurried to the hotel and gave the clerk the letter I wrote before leaving home. I trust he will keep it safe until you and Russ return to Shaniko. A school teacher joined us, going only as far as Bakeoven; her contract had ended for the year so she was traveling to her parents' ranch.

The stars were pinpoints in the dark sky by the time we reached Bakeoven, where we stayed the night. We three shared the last available private room in the two story hotel. Even at the late hour, a kettle of stew was warmed for us, and a loaf of freshly baked bread was sliced. The hotel manager provided some extra quilts and a pillow for a bed on the floor; I felt that the mother and son needed a good rest in the one narrow bed.

Sleep came with difficulty that night, since I was thinking of my long journey ahead. If there are no long delays, I should arrive in Dawson City by the end of August. Does Barrett remember that I am only a plain looking girl? Will we be shy of each other? Sometimes I think, "What am I doing?" I re-read his letter before turning down the lamp, which bolstered my confidence in this decision. I prayed that Mother was not paying too big of a price for helping me leave. Gusts of wind woke us in the purple hours of early dawn; other lodgers were already moving about in the hall. The three of us dressed quickly, made use of the chamber pot behind a small screen, and washed our faces and hands. After joining the stage driver at a hastily prepared breakfast of bread slices spread with butter and jam, washed down with mugs of strong coffee, we gathered our bags to board the stage. Mrs. Carnahan's son was talkative that morning, clutching a huge cinnamon cookie the hotel manager's wife gave him. A shy Indian couple from Warm Springs Reservation took seats inside the stage, and another cowboy perched up with the driver. Two hours after we left Bakeoven, the stage crossed the Deschutes River on a narrow bridge without incident, and the driver stopped for a fresh team.

Little Lester played with his toy soldiers on the stagecoach's floor, a much happier child that day. Rolling thunder echoed from the horizon, but rain skulked on the far-off hills. Our enemy that day was the wind, which buffeted the stage from right to left, and filled the air with dust. Mrs. Carnahan and I tied down the leather window shades; however, we suffered from the heat and stagnant air. The young man from Warm Springs stoically fanned his wife, and we observed that she was carrying a child. I dampened a handkerchief with water from the flask provided by our driver, and offered to sponge her face; later she was able to sleep when the wind slacked. When the driver stopped to give us and the horses a rest, I communicated to the couple that I would help them, and she allowed me to assist her behind the brush to relieve her bladder. I think Mrs. Carnahan was of the opinion I should have left them alone, but it doesn't hurt to be kind. We stopped in Tygh Valley at the Miller Ranch for a change of horses and some food. Young Lester was extremely fatigued by this time (as we all were), and it was a relief when we made our last stop in Dufur. The Dalles was just twelve more miles!

The far-off Cascade Mountain Range dominated the western horizon, and Mount Adams stared at us from the north. Finally we began the steep descent into the Columbia River Gorge. I prayed the driver had his hand on the brake handle, since the road pitched downward for miles. Even the horses seemed relieved when we pulled to a stop in front of the Umatilla Hotel. Mother had arranged for me to stay overnight in a boarding house owned by my friend, Ann Carpenter's grandmother. Mrs. Carnahan and Lester quickly said good-bye when a stern-faced woman identified herself as the doctor's housekeeper, and quickly turned to escort them to their lodging for the night. Mrs. Carnahan suddenly took my hand and whispered, "If you ever meet Archie Carnahan in the north, tell him we love him still." I nodded and wished her good luck, and I really meant it. The young Indian couple had disappeared into the crowd. I paid a drayman to carry my trunk to the railroad depot; carrying my small carpetbag, I followed Mother's directions to the boarding house which was just three blocks from the stage stop.

Mrs. Carpenter greeted me in the three-story building's front hall. She looked very much like Mrs. St. Nicholas with her white hair pinned into a roll on top of her head, and spectacles on her round face. Two pitchers of hot water were brought to my room; after washing thoroughly and changing into a fresh shirtwaist and skirt, I joined the other boarders at a long table loaded with steaming platters of chicken, potatoes, and vegetables, followed by cobblers and cakes, with plenty of hot coffee. I was aware that some of the men at the table were boldly surveying my presence. By dessert I'd had enough of that, so I excused myself and retired to my room. The rest of the evening was spent sitting by my bedroom window, watching barges and small boats navigating up and down the Columbia River. I read Barrett's letter again, then curled up in bed in the darkness, thinking that secretly I was a little excited to have men looking at me.

I asked Mrs. Carpenter to awaken me by five the next morning, to give me time to eat breakfast before boarding the train. When the kind lady knocked, it was almost seven o'clock. She told me to sleep as long as I wished, because the train was delayed by a rock slide, and would not come that day. Later she brought a tray with coffee, eggs, ham, toast and jam. Since I was the only boarder in the house that morning, I was able to soak and wash my hair in the bath tub at the end of the hall. Over a cup of coffee in the kitchen, Mrs. Carpenter's questions about my journey to the far north made me once again realize how far away I am going. My personable landlady disclosed that she came west from Chicago in '56 as a mail-order bride. Mrs. Carpenter hadn't met her husband before she stepped off the stage; her brother had come west a decade earlier, and told his best friend about her. She gently advised me to grow a thick skin to handle remarks and suggestive looks from men, since I have joined a world more theirs than mine.

In the afternoon Mrs. Carpenter asked me to run an errand for her to pick up an order at the butcher shop. On the way I passed several ladies' shops, and was tempted to compare the clothes packed in my trunk to recent fashions. Nickelsen's Booksellers sign caught my eye and since the door was propped open, I ventured inside. There was a distinct smell of lemon oil and vinegar, suggesting the shelves and counters had just been dusted, as well as windows cleaned. Mr. Nickelsen introduced himself; before long we were scanning the shelves for books about the far north. He recommended a copy of Schwatka's *Along Alaska's Great River*, so that I might learn more about my route on the Yukon River. Mrs. Nickelsen suggested that I keep a record of my exciting trip, so I purchased a leather-bound journal, and will try to write in it often.

Mother will be anxious to get some news of my journey so far, so this afternoon I wrote a short letter assuring her my trip was going as planned. I will post mother's letter, and this one for you, in the morning on my on my way to board the train.

Your friend,

Abigail

Callie beamed when Ray said, "Wow, what a story!"

"Yes, I especially love the way she described the stagecoach trip. But then Grandma Abigail was a wonder at writing down her thoughts and observations, all of her life," Callie revealed.

Rosalie asked, "How did her journal's entries differ from the letters?"

"Sadly, Grandma Abby's journal was lost sometime during the years after she moved back to Oregon. That loss upset her very much since I think she spilled her heart onto those pages. When I was about thirty years old, she began dictating her memoir to me, using the letters Alice saved as chronological reminders of events and names. The farther we got into those years in the Yukon, the more she remembered. Abby was quite frank about what happened to her on the hard journey to Dawson City and after she married Barrett. Do you want to read some of the memoir along with the letters?"

"That would be awesome! Are you sure you have the time?" Rosalie exclaimed.

"The question is whether you two have the time," Callie replied.

"We'll make time for it! But first, may I use your 'necessary'?" Ray said.

Callie laughed and pointed down the hall.

I V

. . . .

RAY RETURNED, AND CALLIE BEGAN READING ABI-
gail's memoir which began with the date when she left The Dalles
on the train.

"By June 12, 1898 I was finally headed for Seattle; traveling on the
railroad was certainly faster than a stagecoach journey, but not much
to my liking. It was quite dirty, smoky, and crowded. At least on the
stagecoach, when a call is made, "ladies to the left, gents to the right,"
we could find a clean spot in the forest or prairie to use. The necessary located at the end of our passenger car was terribly soiled and
dark, and lacked a sparkling stream in which to wash. Conditions
on the train I transferred to in Portland, were somewhat improved.
Rumbling along the tracks, it seemed to take forever to get from one
stop to the next. The train made a number of stops, letting off and
picking up passengers at various towns and even small hamlets. I
met a young woman just a few years older than me while waiting in
Portland on my half-day layover. Kate and I shared a table in a small
coffee shop, and talked about our reasons for leaving home. She was
also going to the Klondike, joining a group of entertainers in Seattle
for the journey. Ordinarily I would have considered it scandalous to
be in the company of an actress; however, she was so nice, and our
same destination rather made us of one kind. We had a grand time
on the train to Seattle, talking of families, and sharing dreams for the

future. This train had a dining car, and I felt very grown up sitting at a table with nice white linens and matching utensils. When Kate dozed late in the evening, I looked out the train's window into the blackness, and noticed the lights in homes visible from the tracks. Since I would soon be a wife, I was curious about the families behind those windows: were they happy, in love, fulfilled? I thought of Barrett, and wondered if he was thinking of me."

Callie said, "I feel like Grandma Abigail is right in the room with me, every time I read her letters and memoir. I used to hang on her every word, and she did love to reminisce. By the time Lem and I married, Abigail was living with my momma in Antelope. I'd take the kids over on Saturdays; they would follow Dad around doing chores, and I'd cook or sew and listen to Grandma."

Rosalie asked, "How many years did she stay in the Klondike?"

"Well, let's not jump too far ahead. Here is what she wrote next:

"The route to Seattle was lush and wonderfully green, with tall trees, trailing vines, and colorful meadows. Compared to the high desert of Oregon, it was as if I had journeyed to the opposite side of the world already! When we arrived in Seattle, Kate accompanied me to the hotel where Barrett had reserved a room. Kate was supposed to meet the theatrical company later in the afternoon, but they were delayed, so she stayed the night in my room. I remember at that time the elegant and willowy young actress reminded me of an illustration in a book of Shakespeare's plays I had at home. When we entered the hotel dining room that evening, eyes shifted towards Kate, and tracked her while we were shown our table. I was a little embarrassed but Kate seemed to soak up the attention. I think I was a little jealous, and felt quite dowdy in the plain dress Mother had hand sewn. In my room, we undressed for bed and Kate posed in front of the full-length mirror wearing just her camisole and drawers. Her figure was full and well proportioned, and she laughed when I told her I wished I had her shape. She pulled me to the mirror and as we stood side by side, she said I had a very nice figure for a young woman. Kate was taller than me by two or three inches, which seemed to be mostly in her legs. Our waists measured the same, but hers looked tinier since her bust was larger. Kate's hair was dark brown and wouldn't even be tamed by a net, not that she really tried. I called my hair a plain brown, but Kate said it was definitely maple colored, and she admired its heavy smooth waves. I had never examined my physical appearance so; usually a cursory glance when I ran a brush through my hair was all the attention I gave myself. In fact, I'd never seen myself full length, all at once. Kate had a cute turned up nose, pale skin and large blue eyes. Her shoulders were so white they looked like marble. Having worked outdoors so much, I had a 'farmer's tan': brown face and hands, but my shoulders were also white like Kate's. She said that as a youngster, she occasionally had trouble with blemishes on her face; she started using an oatmeal scrub, and her complexion became as smooth as a peach in cream. I had always had good skin, except for the permanent tan. Kate tried to convince me that Barrett probably picked me for my looks, but down deep I felt that was not his reason. We talked late into the night, and the next morning we bade each other 'Good-bye and good luck.' I wondered if I would ever see her again.

"Seattle was swarming with thousands of would-be gold seekers and hundreds of vendors on the streets hawking their supplies and guide books for the Yukon. Shops advertised complete outfits which a person supposedly needed to make the journey. Barrett had reserved passage for me on the brand new ship *St. Paul* to St. Michaels, located on the western coast of Alaska Territory. From there the plan was to board a small sternwheeler that would push almost 2000 miles up the Yukon River to the city where my new husband waited. The first morning after my arrival in Seattle, I hurried to the shipping agent's office to collect my ticket and confirm the time and date of departure. You can just imagine my disappointment when agent Brooks abruptly informed me that the *St. Paul* was sailing from San Francisco instead of Seattle; he promised to find another passage for me and the several crates of supplies Barrett had ordered. I still had to shop for items not available at home, and as promised, Barrett had a draft waiting at Seattle First Bank to cover all expenses. I knew that the winters were extremely cold in the Yukon, with the thermometer reaching at least forty below. Barrett told me to purchase a thick fur parka, with a hood that could be drawn up so that only my eyes would be exposed. At Kline's Clothiers I bought a beautiful beaver skin parka, trimmed with wolverine fur. Mr. Kline said the wolverine trim would not freeze from my breath moisture, when the temperature reached sub-zero temperatures. He also advised me to purchase two pairs of boots: one pair, knee-high and lined with fur; the other pair, waterproof. I also bought a pair of canvas trousers, lined with wool, and long johns to wear under my skirts. At that time I had no idea how many months of the year I would wear those ugly long johns. I finally received a message from Mr. Brooks assuring me that I had a berth on a re-commissioned whaler named *Aleutian Storm*. When I went to his office, the agent admitted the accommodations were stark compared to the *St. Paul's*, but for me and two hundred others, it was our last chance to reach the Yukon while it was ice-free. He advised me to take linens and blankets, and he had it on authority that an experienced cook had been hired. One of Mr. Brook's assistants mentioned that meals on the old converted ships were sometimes unpredictable, so I purchased a supply of tinned and dried foods. Later, while at sea eating from a monotonous menu provided onboard, I thanked heaven above for that advice. It would be a 4,000 mile journey from Seattle to St. Michaels, and was estimated to take nearly three weeks, barring mishaps, with a stop in Dutch Harbor.

"I wrote to Mother and Alice, asking them to not worry about me. I made friends with two ladies in the hotel who were going to Dawson to open a dress shop, and they had also bought passage on the *Aleutian Storm*. Although Dawson City was isolated in the far north and in many ways reported to be very primitive, these women told me that some prominent residents enjoyed an atmosphere of high society, with formal dances and fancy dinners."

Callie opened another envelope and read a short message written to Alice the day before they sailed.

June 16, 1898
Seattle, Wash.

Dear Alice,

I have already seen and experienced so much in these last two weeks, that I am feeling more confident in my decision to join Barrett. Please do not worry about me. We board in the morning, and leave on the tide. I believe I can post another letter to you from Dutch Harbor.

Your friend,

Abigail

"Grandma Abigail spent a small fortune on these letters, and many times Alice had to pay more when they arrived, but isn't it great that she took the time to write them?" Callie asked.

Rosalie nodded, and Ray said, "I wonder what possessed Alice to keep them? Most letters get tossed, which is a shame when you think of it."

"I believe Grandma Alice might have been living vicariously thru

Abigail," answered Callie. "Once Alice married, she was expected to maintain a gracious home, in a rather stifled society. Grandpa Russ never really approved of Abigail; I think he was a little afraid she would bring out a mischievous side in Alice."

"Whatever Alice's reasons, she probably had no idea what they would mean to later generations, I'm sure," said Rosalie.

Callie added, "Toward the end of her life, I think she did realize their importance. I've always treasured their value as historical documents."

"I'm amazed at Abigail's memory of tiny details, so many years after the fact," Rosalie said.

Callie agreed, "I think because she originally wrote often in her journal, and read through it later in her life, until it was lost, the memories were kept alive. Next, Grandma Abby described in her memoir the exciting voyage to Dutch Harbor."

"By June 20th our ship had battled high seas and gale winds for two days, and at times I feared we wouldn't survive. I had never been so frightened in my life. To prevent being slammed against the walls of our cabins, we took to our bunks; during the worst hours of the storm, I even tied myself to the bunk rails. Hour after hour, I was jerked back and forth, and found myself following the ship's movements, unable to stop repeating in my mind, 'Up, down, roll, slosh' which did nothing but add to my nausea. Just about everyone except the crew was sick, with no chance of cleaning up the mess until the storm ended. Unlike some of the nicer vessels, this ship has no stewards; cabin mates were the only people who remotely cared about each other. I was very lucky that my cabin companions were the two ladies I met at the hotel. Esther Cohen and Molly Green approached me right after we boarded in Seattle, about sharing their tiny stateroom, instead of having to bunk in the large dormitory below deck.

Esther discovered that our captain was Jewish, as they are, and she convinced him that we could use the ship doctor's larger cabin, since we were among the very few women on board and besides, there was no doctor hired for this trip. We paid extra for a member of the crew to build another bunk; our trunks and bags covered the entire floor, which we climbed over to reach the door. A crude toilet was located in a tiny closet at the end of the hall, but we knew there was no such luxury below: passengers from the dormitory had to come up to the main deck to a box affair that hung over the stern that served as their open-air toilet. Along our hall were the captain's and first mate's quarters, a small cabin for chief engineer and the cook, and a larger room for six other crew members. I will give the captain credit for checking on us occasionally, although his time was limited for pleasantries.

"The cook prepared two meals a day: a late morning bowl of hot cereal with bread and butter; around five o'clock a supper of beans with bacon or boiled potatoes with chipped beef was served, and always stewed apples. With the beans we got cornbread with lots of butter, otherwise, the bread served was coarse and tough, best when toasted and buttered. Miss Cohen and Mrs. Green appreciated my supply of dried fruits and tinned foods, since they had not been advised to bring any. Mid-afternoons, if the seas were not pitching us around, we perched on our baggage and share a small meal from my stores. One day a young boy wandered to our deck from quarters below, and stopped to stare through our half-open cabin door. We invited him in, and during Jimmy Jensen's meal with us he said, with wide-open eyes of excitement, he was accompanying his father to Dawson City so they could return home rich. We filled an emptied cracker tin with sweet meats, dried fruits, crackers and canned sardines when he said he had to get back to his father. I suggested that he might eat just a few bites from the box each day, and he agreed;

however, we learned that he promptly shared the treats with his father and bunk mates.

"One evening I opened our cabin door and Jimmy stumbled inside, burying his head in my shawl. 'Oh, Miss Parker!' he cried, 'Help my daddy! He's hurtin' ever so bad!' Following Jimmy below decks, I halted at the doorway, unsure how to approach the problem. The mass of men parted as we made our way through the unwashed crowd. I questioned Mr. Jensen first, and then asked a man to probe his abdomen. A horse doctor was on board, but one of the men said he had been drunk in his own bunk for two days. You can imagine my relief when it appeared the pain was not situated where an infected appendix would be. Using what I knew from growing up far from a doctor and watching Mother, I treated him with castor oil, and within a day, Lars Jensen was much improved. That chance meeting became a moment that affected many decisions I made over time.

"Gold fever was an ailment affecting all passengers on the vessel. Twice a day my cabin mates and I ventured amidships to the galley for our meals, mingling with men and a few women who were certain they would soon make their fortunes in the far north. Most were prospectors, but I also met photographers, dentists, assayers, merchants, cooks, inn keepers, actors, gamblers and bankers. The men were very polite for the most part, and some were already homesick for their loved ones back home. When the weather permitted, everyone stayed on deck to breathe fresh air, avoiding the stale atmosphere in the dark dormitory. I couldn't imagine how claustrophobic it must have been below decks. At least our little cabin boasted a plate-sized port hole, which we could open for ventilation. Lars and Jimmy Jensen made a habit of joining me (with my permission) on strolls around the ship, although Esther Cohen disapproved. Lars cut a nice figure with his broad shoulders, sandy hair, and small mustache over a sweet smile. When I walked and talked with him, I felt special and pretty; at night, I reread Barrett's letter, and felt very guilty for enjoying another man's company.

"By June 26 I felt like I had been travelling for many months, and some days I wondered if I were doing the right thing. Molly Green had been a widow ten years, and when she spoke about her husband and their content life together, I could hear the emotion in her voice. I didn't feel that way about Barrett yet. I wondered if Alice ever questioned whether she loved Russ enough. I hoped we wouldn't have a child right away, since I wanted to show Barrett how much help I could be with the church school.

"Finally, the captain announced that we would dock in Dutch Harbor, Alaska Territory, in the Aleutian Islands. I prayed that a letter from Barrett would be waiting for me there."

Callie said, "Grandma Abby was really beginning to doubt what she was doing, but unlike some passengers, who had already decided to find passage back to Seattle when they arrived in Dutch Harbor, she steadfastly clung to her promise to join Barrett."

"As of June 28, our ship was still waiting its turn at the coal dock, waiting for a barge from Seattle to resupply. There must have been fifteen ships at anchor in the harbor, housing 2000 or more adventurers. Some of the men from the *Aleutian Storm* disembarked and hired a skiff to take them ashore for a day. Lars Jensen had joined several men who walked through the swampy ground to the village of Unalaska, three miles away. He described a small settlement, with Russian Orthodox and Methodist churches. Disease took the lives of many natives in prior years, and an orphanage was run by the Methodist. Dozens of tents were pitched between the village and Dutch Harbor, occupied by Dawson bound travelers who had been emptied from ships that wanted to return to Seattle quickly for more Klondike passengers. These poor souls were affected terribly by the frequent rain, snow and fog. Mr. Jensen questioned several men who said they had been promised passage to Dawson City on one of the newly constructed flat-bottomed steamers that were towed to the mouth of the Yukon a few days later. In our case, the *Aleutian Storm* had contracted to deliver us to St. Michaels, at the mouth of the Yukon River, where shallow-draft steamers bringing homebound miners downstream to the ships, took on passengers for the return river journey to Dawson City.

"The second day we were in Dutch Harbor, a merry group from a nearby ship came alongside in a skiff, and invited our passengers to an evening of entertainment. When I peered over the side, one of the women onboard began waving and calling 'Abigail, Abigail!' I was shocked, and a little embarrassed, when everyone looked in my direction; my friend from the railroad trip, Kate, stood up in the skiff and smiled so genuinely that I had to return the greeting. She yelled that we should meet soon; when I nodded, she offered (loudly) to come aboard the next morning. Of course I was glad to see her, although my cabin mates disapproved of Kate's profession. We had a wonderful visit which served to lift my spirits. She was so full of life, and took what came along with nary a concern. Kate questioned my motives for marrying Barrett, even though she knew of my problems at home. Declaring that she would never marry without love, Kate recognized my discomfort and quickly assured me that everything will work out just fine. Her company of actors had arranged to rent a theater of sorts in Dawson City for their productions. Kate enjoyed singing and dancing the most; however the troupe also put on plays where she was pushed into acting a part. I knew my family might have been upset with my acceptance of Kate's profession, but I believed most would appreciate her good heart under the face paint. Kate was an astute young woman, and made it plain that she understood how Barrett's standing in the community would prevent our friendship in public. I protested, but she patted my hand and shook her head; we agreed to find a secret method to keep up with each other. I think I liked Kate from the first because she was so brave, and wasn't locked into a particular role in life."

Callie put the memoir on her lap, and gave a little conspirator's smile. "Oh, they did manage to see each other. Without Kate's friendship, Abigail said she wouldn't have lasted two months in Dawson City."

"Just as he promised, a letter from Barrett was waiting for me at the remote station, brought down the river from Dawson City right after the ice released its hold on the route, and taken further to Dutch Harbor. The letter I received in May in Prineville had been written in March, taken up the frozen Yukon River by dog sled to Lake LeBarge; from there, the mail was transported over the mountain barrier to Skagway, an ice-free port. All winter, ships from west coast cities plied the waters, delivering gold seekers who could not wait until summer, who took their chances ascending Chilkoot Pass to access the Yukon. These ships not only took supplies and adventurers to Skagway, they returned to the United States with dispatches and disillusioned men and women. This new letter from Barrett boosted my courage; his attitude was so positive about our marriage, that I found it infectious! He enclosed a photograph of himself, looking so serious and handsome. Sometimes I thought I didn't deserve such a man.

"Barrett wrote that we now had our own home, and would not have to lodge in a noisy rooming house. With the help of friends he had completed a two room log cabin, which boasted a plank floor. Having a real floor made of lumber was a luxury in the Yukon, where milling the trees was a slow process and very expensive. An iron stove for the cabin was onboard my ship, part of the supplies for the church that Barrett ordered from Seattle. I had purchased linens, towels, pillows, rugs and a down comforter in Seattle, which were tightly packed around a few dishes and pots, also crated and in the hold of the ship. Barrett wrote he had accumulated some furniture that was left behind by Dawson City residents, when they decided to return home. Some of them left with bags of gold, and others left after their belongings were sold to purchase a ticket to Seattle. At the time Barrett's letter was written, two-hundred men and women a day were pouring into the Klondike region; that number would double by the time I arrived. The population of Dawson City reached thirty thousand in a matter of weeks. Food was in short supply the previous winter for those who stayed, therefore Barrett's crates from Seattle included 1,000 pounds of dried and tinned meats, fruits, nuts and sweets, plus flour, coffee, and sugar. Barrett told me that in Dawson eggs cost three dollars each, an apple was one dollar, and a sack of flour was fifty dollars. As long as the steamers were able to bring supplies up the Yukon, restaurants offered a bounty of gourmet meals, from stuffed duck to escargot. A plain meal of beans, bacon and sourdough bread cost $2.50, a twenty-five cent meal in Prineville at that time!

"I tried to imagine what Dawson looked like from Barrett's description. He wrote that the streets were ankle deep in mud when they weren't frozen, and ramshackle dwellings were spread over the low hills with no organized plan for streets or alleys. However, there were two hospitals, Canadian Royal Mounted Police Headquarters, opera house and many shops. Although the town contained numerous dance halls and saloons, law was upheld by the Canadian authorities, and Barrett said there was very little crime. Newspapers in Oregon and Washington wrote such wild stories of the Gold Rush, that I had a notion Dawson would be terribly lawless. Barrett's assurance of the opposite situation was a great relief. While miners were not robbed of their fortunes, gold nuggets were gambled away, or spent on women in the saloons; fortunes were won and lost many times each night. Barrett assured me that I would not be exposed to these rough crowds, because our cabin sat next to the church. He wouldn't have approved of the men and women with whom I passed time on the long voyage north, but I didn't judge them. Most of the men onboard were polite and gracious, especially when they heard that I was joining my fiancé, the reverend. My future husband said he did not want me to be burdened by housework so he hired a young half-breed woman named Etta to help with that so I would have more time for the church school. Barrett was so anxious for me to arrive in Dawson City."

"I always thought that Dawson City was a hotbed of crime and unsavory characters. This is a complete surprise to me!" Ray said.

"I know what you mean. So much has been written that makes the Klondike seem more sinister than it was," Callie agreed, as she opened another envelope.

July 5, 1898
Dutch Harbor, Alaska Territory

Dear Alice,

On Independence Day Captain Davis held a ceremony for us to join the crew in patriotic songs and dance. The few women on board stayed in the background, watching men dance with each other. Lars and Jimmy joined the fun and danced until they fell exhausted on the deck. It was nice to see them having a good time. Kate's ship re-coaled and headed north yesterday.

For the last few days we have watched a distant volcano spew ash and smoke into the sky. During the darkest part of the night, Dutch Harbor visitors can see the red glow of lava on the volcano's flanks, a wondrous phenomenon. It is located farther west in the Aleutian Chain of islands, so we will not have to sail past it when we leave for St. Michaels.

A newspaper published in Dawson has circulated throughout the ship, which includes several photographs: a muddy river bank with boats of all sizes, saloons made of canvas with rough plank fronts, and a winter scene of freight being hauled in sleds pulled by a team of malamutes. I am so excited to join that strange world.

The ship's cook purchased some fresh fish which has helped infuse excitement at the dinner bell. Life aboard ship is actually quite boring; Esther and Molly spend hours in our cabin, designing hats and dresses they will make once we arrive in Dawson. The book I bought in The Dalles about the Yukon River is proving to be a wonderful way to learn about our journey. When my friends are bent over their handwork, I read aloud which helps to pass the time onboard. When I'm tired of reading or walking the deck, I pick up my knitting needles and have made two pairs of stockings so far. Mother always sewed most of our clothes, but she taught me the basic stitches, so I get by. My seamstress friends are teaching me about patterns and different fabrics; this skill might come in handy while we are in the north. During this time, I've had my monthly which is an inconvenient thing on an ocean voyage. Esther secured a small bucket in which we can soak the rags, stowed under my bunk. Surely I will be in my own home before the next month. Men are so lucky to not have such an impediment to a free lifestyle.

Oh, the captain has just informed us that the ship will re-coal in the morning. We will be on our way to St. Michaels by noon! I will say good-bye for now and dispatch this letter with the afternoon mail.

Your friend,

Abigail

Callie placed the letter in her lap, and peered over her reading glasses at Rosalie and Ray. Each was visibly affected by the contents of such a descriptive piece of history.

Rosalie said, "I always thought of the Klondike gold rush in terms of men climbing the icy mountain pass near Skagway. Ray, did you know that folks took ships clear out past the Aleutian Islands to get to the Yukon River?"

"The only thing I knew about the Aleutians was its being invaded by the Japanese during World War II; and I never even heard of St. Michaels, Alaska," Ray replied.

Callie explained, "There were many ways to get to the gold strikes along the Yukon River and in the Klondike District. Grandma Abby told me about the prospectors she met up there, and their stories of hardships along the trail. Some used the all Canadian route, overland from Edmonton, and many climbed over the Chilkoot Pass at Skagway. That route was particularly grueling, since the Canadian Mounties required each person coming into the Yukon Territory to haul one ton of food with them. Each prospector had to make about 20 trips up and down that pass, just to get their supplies to the check station at the crest."

Ray exclaimed, "That's what I remember reading!"

"Abigail was fortunate to have had her passage paid on the ocean and river voyages. In today's money, her fare cost close to six thousand dollars," Callie added.

"Oh, my!" said Rosalie. "Those people were risking so much: their lives plus perhaps all the money they could scrape together."

"Yes, but each thought that he might be the one to strike the mother lode," Callie laughed.

Ray asked, "Was the Yukon River route well mapped?"

"Actually, river steamers had been running up and down the Yukon since the 1870's, and the Russians had explored the region and established trading posts along the river before that. Hudson's Bay Company also set up shop, but was replaced by the Alaska Commercial Company. At the same time, missionaries were intent on saving souls in the north, so settlements sprang up with schools, missions, and hospitals."

Rosalie asked, "So you learned all this from your Grandmother?"

"I am here to tell you that she shared all she could remember about the Klondike and her own life during that time," Callie said. "Reading her old letters jogs my old memory!"

"I am ready to hear about her trip up the river!" Ray said.

Rosalie interjected, "I am anxious to find out what happens once she gets to Dawson City!"

"Let's see, Abby's ship was just leaving Dutch Harbor.

V

. . . .

"THE VOYAGE FROM DUTCH HARBOR TO ST. MI-
chaels was a challenge for our overloaded ark. Miserable days of
bone chilling dampness kept passengers in their bunks, huddled under quilts. For two days it rained hard; the captain was overheard
instructing a crew member to keep the bilge pumps manned at all
times. Esther Cohen suffered from a stomach ailment after we left
Dutch Harbor; Molly and I were quite worried a whole day and night,
but Esther slowly recovered. Lars described the horrific scene below
decks, since many passengers apparently suffered from the same illness. One old man accompanying his son to the Klondike died. Lars
and his son Jimmy were alright. It was rumored that some of the fish
served onboard had gone bad.

"As the ship sailed north everyone noticed the days were longer
and the nights shorter. I found it odd to wake in the morning light,
and discover it was only three o'clock. Passengers had to remind
themselves to go to bed, even though the sun was still shining at
eleven. By the time we reached the Yukon River, nights provided just
two hours of darkness. There was so much to learn about the foreign
world in the north.

"On July 14, 1898, as we steamed across the Yukon Delta, north to
St. Michaels, the ocean became so shallow that the ship stuck fast on
the mud; however, when the tide rose a few feet, the ship once more

made progress. The delta stretches many miles offshore, formed from the silt washed down the mighty river. While waiting to float off the mud, I leaned on the rail, watching debris float past, and soon Lars joined me. He said that Jimmy was asleep and certainly didn't let the daylight impact his schedule like the rest of us. I told Lars that I could get very turned around with the days and nights. When I asked him what he thought the dark winters were like, he said 'Probably boring!' We talked late into the long purple twilight.

"Lars had been a commercial artist back home, but like everyone else on the ship, he planned to dig for gold, even if he had to work for someone else. He told me, "I found myself unemployed after working ten years for the same company. When we heard about the gold strike, I decided that I would give it a try. It took almost every cent I had to pay for the trip." I asked if his wife was dead, and he just said she wasn't well, and lived with her sister. I could only reply that I was sure he would find a way to make a living, but if he and Jimmy needed help along the way, not to forget they had a friend in Dawson. I was sure Barrett would feel the same. Finally I said that my cabin mates would wonder where I was at the late hour. Lars escorted me to the passageway, and watched until I was safely inside. Tempers and anxiety had been poking their ugly heads up among the passengers the last few days, of which Lars was quite aware living below decks. He told me that several men had made suggestive comments about the 'lovely lady', and cautioned me to be careful.

"Once anchored off St. Michaels, the anxious wait for our stern-wheel steamer began. At first the ship anchored close to shore, but the mosquitoes made it impossible to stay on deck; they even found their way into the cabins, which led to sleepless nights for everyone. These particular mosquitoes were huge, and attacked in large swarms which, according to old-timers, could drive moose and caribou over cliffs while trying to escape. Captain Davis moved the *Aleutian Storm* farther off shore, which finally gave us some relief from the pests! Molly had lapsed into a melancholic mood; Esther thought the journey was proving more difficult than she had anticipated. I just hoped that once we began the river voyage, where stops at settlements along the way might replace the monotony of the ocean trip, she would revive. From listening to my friends discuss their business I understood that the two women had invested all their savings into starting the ladies' clothing store in Dawson; so they too had risked much to gain more. One evening Lars knocked on our cabin door, and invited us to join him and Jimmy mid-ship for musical entertainment presented by a group of Irishmen. It was rousing fun, enjoyed by all! I told Lars that Molly and Esther's laughter was like a tonic for me.

"After Molly and Esther retired to the cabin that night, Lars told me more about his wife. He convinced her that he should go north for a year, and gamble on making a gold strike. Myra could live with her sister, but it was not possible for Jimmy to stay with her. The only thing to do was bring Jimmy with him. I couldn't understand how a mother could let that happen, but I believed Lars. Onboard the ship, Lars schooled his son an hour or two each day, and I offered to help with some lessons. My books were packed in crates stowed below, inaccessible until we reached Dawson; however, we made do. Lars showed us several sketches he drew of the ship and Dutch Harbor; soon he had earned a little money penciling candid portraits of passengers for their wives or parents back home. I so enjoyed spending evenings talking with Lars, and I was flattered he was interested in what I said.

"Captain Davis assured me that he would see that we ladies had a real stateroom on the river steamer, which could carry one hundred people comfortably. The steamer was equipped to push a barge along in front, which would hold the remainder of the passengers who would sleep on cots under a canvas roof. I asked the captain which vessel Lars and Jimmy would be assigned since they wanted to continue with the school lessons. He said they would also travel on the steamer, which caused Esther to clap her hands together, and all three of us laughed. Jimmy had a way of brightening our days.

"The time it took to reach Dawson City was a journey of patience, which chafed everyone's nerves. There was too much time for dreaming and worrying, although we three women kept our hands busy. I would have paid a large reward for a real bath and clothes that weren't rinsed in sea water. Imagine my delight to learn that Kate was also in the harbor, awaiting her steamer. She visited one afternoon, with Molly and Esther even accepting Kate's invitation to dine from her basket full of meat pies and muffins. Her ship's accommodations and meals were much superior to what was served on the *Aleutian Storm*. Esther prepared a pot of Chinese tea from our dwindling food stash. The ladies absolutely glowed under Kate's approval of the dress designs they shared with her. How could they not appreciate her offer to bring her friends to their shop; yet I knew they were conflicted."

Callie stopped to make a pot of coffee, and dished up generous helpings of her peach cobbler.

"Ray, would you like to make it a la mode?"

"Oh, why not?" he chuckled, as Rosalie raised her eyebrows and declined the ice cream.

When everyone was finished, Callie opened the next envelope.

July 22, 1898
St. Michaels, Alaska Territory

Dear Alice,

Remember last year on this day, when we celebrated my birthday? Since Jim was rounding up cattle in the mountains for a few days, I invited friends to our place, and Mother outdid herself with food and cake. I have not felt so carefree since then. The oddest thing is that I feel five years older this year; must be because so much has happened in these last few months. No one knows so much about me as you; please don't forget about your Klondike friend, and write me often. Send your letters to Mrs. Barrett Rogers, in care of the First Methodist Church in Dawson City, Y.T. Canada.

Kate's steamer completed loading passengers and cargo yesterday and early this morning the *M/V Texas* left, plunging through the fog to rendezvous with the mouth of the Yukon. Our steamer arrived today; already, the huge cargo nets have lifted Seattle-bound crates from the hold, and transferred them to an ocean-going ship. As soon as our Dawson-bound cargo and passengers are loaded, we will head upriver, probably within two days. The last leg of my journey is about to begin! This letter will be the last I can send until we reach Holy Cross, hundreds of miles up the mighty river unless a steamer heading downstream to St. Michaels agrees to carry our dispatches.

Your friend,
Abigail

"After a week on the river, I had to admit that the wonders I experienced during my sea voyage were just a prelude to this part of my voyage. Our steamer, the *M/V Olive May*, chugged steadily against the current of the majestic river. The mouth of the Yukon River is twenty or thirty miles wide and I am still mystified how the captain knew where to start! As we steamed up a channel, Captain Jones had to dodge debris that resembled long islands of trees and shrubs. Just underneath the water's surface, logs bobbed up and down, presenting hazards in the steamer's path. A crew member stood alert on the bow, making soundings with a rope and weight, and calling out warnings to Captain Jones. The *M/V Olive May* was wood-fired, so every two days we pulled ashore to refuel from the stacks of four-foot long logs cut by local Indians during the winter. The crew members, who loaded many cords of wood at each stop, must have had thick skin, since the back-breaking work was made more difficult by hordes of mosquitoes. While the refueling took place, we three women retreated to our cabin to escape the maddening pests. Once the steamer was back into the middle of the river, which had narrowed to about a mile, we could once again walk along the decks. Sometimes, Captain Jones had to crowd the shore, so when outside our cabin we wore hats with mosquito netting sewn around the brims. With the lower end tucked into the necks of our long-sleeved dresses, and hands protected with gloves, we were able to be outdoors unless the horde of pests were so thick on the veils it became impossible to see where we stepped! The barge passengers spent much of their time resting on cots with netting draped over a rope above them, and edges tucked under the bedding. When the river was buffeted by stiff winds, it gave passengers a chance to move freely about the steamer and barge, since mosquitoes and other flying pests were blown aside.

"Lars and Jimmy went ashore at one stop, and met several gold seekers who were looking for passage to Dawson City, after their small boats were not able to make headway against the strong river current. Captain Jones took five of their number aboard, and came to regret it. Lars was so very considerate to us ladies, by helping in small ways. Occasionally our steamer made stops at the mouths of small tributaries to collect fresh water; Lars hauled water onboard for our personal use in washing clothes and ourselves. In return, we took care of his and Jimmy's laundry. The water in the mighty Yukon River was filled with silt, which left clothes washed in it dingy and a glass of water gritty. Freshets fed by mountain snow fields which merged into the river provided passengers with the sweetest of drinking water.

"The scenery that swept along the low slopes extending from the river bank was truly breathtaking; gold and green aspens interspersed with red foliage seemed to be part of a master's landscape painting. Tall spruce trees and white barked birch dotted the upper hillsides for as far as one could see. Small native villages perched right on the river banks provided an education in the lives of indigenous peoples. Some were wearing skins, and some wore white man's clothing. Children were usually half naked, with greasy faces and hands. The smell of the village announced itself before we came within sight of a campfire; drying fish, dogs, and human filth violated our senses. I kept telling myself that those humans were simply ignorant of a better way of life. I knew that Barrett's mission in life included these people and their salvation; I prayed I could be as effective within the school.

"Captain Jones delivered a short sermon each Sunday, for those who wanted to attend. I was surprised at first with the numbers who stayed in their bunks, especially on the barge. Molly and Esther did not attend, of course, since the message was centered on the teachings of Christ. Those sweet women surprised me with a new bonnet of dove gray taffeta with pale yellow silk roses for my trousseau, but I wore it to the sermon that first Sunday. Jimmy always accompanied me, but Lars did not. I hoped that in Dawson City, he would attend Barrett's church. Frequently our steamer met boats of all descriptions floating downstream. Warnings were shouted to us, 'Go back! No good claims left!' Or 'Save your money, Dawson is full of poor men!' Most of the gold seekers on our steamer were not deterred in the least. Lars didn't want to believe he was too late to make a claim. For his and Jimmy's sakes, I hoped he was right; but I was afraid those men were telling the truth.

"A barge passenger fell overboard one night; although a tremendous effort was made to recover him, the swift current sucked him down. I hoped that someone knew how to contact his family, so they wouldn't wonder and wait for his return. The Alaska Territory seemed to be a place where life was on a tightrope: one minute you were just fine, and the next you were dead. I wondered when a man was close to death, struggling against a current or fighting to survive the cold, did he have time for any regrets?

"Early the next morning we arrived at Holy Cross, where the Catholic mission reigns on one side of the river, and the Indian village on the other. Captain Jones stood at the deck rail with Lars and me, enlightening us on the history. The mission was established in 1888 as the base for the Catholic Church in the Alaska Territory, which provided both a day school and a boarding school. Captain Jones didn't have a high opinion of the bishop, who was heavy-handed in his induction of the Indians to Christianity. He said the younger generation had accepted the church teachings; however, the elders continued to follow the old traditions, which continually led to conflicts. Most of them relied on a shaman to treat illnesses, and spurned modern medicine. Most Indian women were worked like slaves, but accepted it since they knew no other way. There was a lot of pressure on the younger people to follow the ancient teachings, but countless numbers adopted the new way of life, with white man's rules.

"Alaska Commercial Company operated a store and trading post in Holy Cross, and that day several Indian men unloaded some crates off our steamer. Lars pointed out that two of the five men our steamer picked up a few days earlier were pushing an Indian man around, and provoked him into a fight. Captain Jones quickly dispatched two crew members ashore to break it up, collaring the troublemakers. They received a warning that the next time would be the last day onboard this vessel. Lars suspected they had something to do with the drowning the previous night; however, no one came forward as a witness.

"Boat traffic on the Yukon was very active, and occasionally we came upon wrecked hulls and more stranded prospectors. One group of five men and three women decided to pan for gold right where they landed. Captain Jones told us they seemed to have all of the wrong equipment, none of what they needed, and would find no gold at that location. The news that reached the U.S. after the gold strikes in 1897 was so sensational that men assumed every stream would produce nuggets. There were some hugely successful claims, but it was a very limited area where gold was found.

"Lars sketched a portrait of me to send to my family in Oregon. He suggested a pose where I stood at the rail, and looked across the great river. Jimmy judged it to be a perfect likeness, but I didn't believe I was as pretty as Lars portrayed. My hair was just plain brown, not even a dark shade, and I never did like my nose, even though it was just like Mother's. At least my brown eyes were large with long lashes. At that age, my figure wasn't very rounded yet, but Mother had said after I had children, that would change; she was right.

"Mrs. Green gave me some delicate batiste material to make a nightgown. It wasn't very practical with a frigid winter ahead, but she said every bride needed a new gown on her wedding night. That subject had been pushed to the back of my mind on purpose; but I realized right then that I really didn't know Barrett very well at all."

Callie stopped reading to say, "My daughter has Grandma Abigail's portrait hanging in her house. Actually, she was quite pretty, even when she was a great-grandmother. I always wanted to look like that portrait."

Rosalie said, "Hmmm, I'm wondering if she married Barrett? It sure seems like she had doubts."

"Oh, there's lots of water to flow under the bridge yet!" Callie informed them, which only piqued Rosalie's interest. "An accident happened a few days after the steamer left Holy Cross that always gave me goose bumps when Grandma Abigail spoke of it."

"One clear night when the steamer was slowly maneuvering in a channel along the south shore, my friends and I were sitting near the steamship's bow, just enjoying the quiet evening. Suddenly Lars ran forward and pointed to an orange glow just visible beyond a bend in the river. When the scene came into view, it was horrifying: a small steamer was fully engulfed in flames with passengers in the water and on shore screaming and yelling for help. The *Olive May* pushed the barge past the conflagration and was made fast to the shore. Before landing, men were already jumping into the river, pulling injured and scared passengers to safety. I ran to our cabin and gathered linens and blankets as fast as I could. When I ran down the gangplank already thrown onshore, I saw Lars tearing burned clothing from a dazed man's back. Luckily, one of the burning steamboat's passengers was a doctor who had not been injured; I assisted him by placing strips of clean cloth on burns after they were cleaned and covered with a greasy ointment. The Alaskan twilight through the night was a godsend, but it also unmasked the gruesome scene for all to see. Two steamers, *Hamilton* and *Rosanna Belle* came up on the scene, and agreed to take the uninjured passengers on to Dawson City. Finally, about 7 a.m., I returned to the *Olive May* to wash the blood and soot off my body. Lars followed me up the gang plank, anxious to check on Jimmy, who had been ordered to stay with Molly throughout the night.

"Lars asked if I was alright, and he put his hands on my shoulders when we reached the passageway. 'Just shaken by what I have seen tonight,' I said. 'Is it wrong to feel so thankful that it was them instead of us? He replied, 'I hope not, because I feel the same. Those poor souls.'

"Lars added, 'Captain Jones says we aren't far from Anvik, which has a mission with medical help. It's the best we can do for them."

"Neither of us seemed ready to part, and in a moment I realized we were standing very close, and then Lars moved his hands to my waist. I didn't know how to react; after all, he was married, and I was promised.

"You are a very pretty woman, Abigail. I hope you know that," Lars whispered. I pulled away and told him he should fetch Jimmy, but I could still feel his touch an hour later.

VI

. . . .

"OUR STEAMER PULLED UP TO THE DOCK IN ANVIK
on August 4th. Reverend Smyth was in charge of the Episcopal mission at that time; his wife had trained as a nurse in Seattle, so they
provided some medical treatments for locals. The doctor who was
headed to Dawson City said he would stay in Anvik until the injured
passengers improved enough to be moved. I learned later on that
Reverend Smyth tried to persuade Dr. Pearson to stay permanently;
however he had a contract with the new St. Mary's Hospital in Dawson City and I saw him often during the time I lived there.

"At this point in my voyage I felt as if the days dragged on forever,
and I would never get to Dawson City. Barrett's letters were worn
through at the folds, becoming very tattered since I read them at least
once a day. Esther, who had never been married, became impatient
one night when I kept the kerosene lamp brightly lit while reading
the letters. Molly cluck-clucked at her, and I heard no more about it.
I had a feeling that Molly knew what had passed between Lars and
me, or perhaps I was just feeling guilty.

"Four days later, just before arriving in Nulato, our steamer suffered a broken rudder. Captain Jones solicited help from some of the
men to help the crew position the steamer along the river bank. The
mosquitoes almost drove them mad until a stiff breeze came up in
the afternoon. A woman onboard the barge, which was anchored a

short distance away, became ill. She was moaning terribly when two men carried her to the steamer asking for help. Right away, Molly announced, 'This young lady is having a baby!' The poor woman was a simple person, and said she didn't know she was with child until the pains began. One of the men with her was an uncle, who became very angry with the news since he had brought her along to be a cook at one of the mining camps. Our cabin was too crowded to deal with a baby's birth, so the Captain put her in the first mate's room. Molly took over, and a few hours later a tiny, stillborn boy was delivered. It was very sad, but I don't believe that girl could have taken care of a baby."

August 9, 1898
Nulato, Alaska Territory

Dear Alice,

Our steamer stopped in Nulato this afternoon, to take on wood and drop off supplies for the new Catholic Mission. It is quite a busy village, and even has a post office! Since writing you last, I have seen a steamer burn to the waterline, nursed injured passengers, helped deliver a baby that died, and fought off the biggest mosquitoes in the world!

One of our passengers purchased half a dozen sled dogs from an Indian man in the village; they all looked exactly the same: massive, fluffy malamutes. I overheard him say he had to pay one hundred dollars apiece, but will double his money in Dawson City. The snarling, yipping team is kept tied near the bow of the barge, and their owner is paying another passenger to feed and care for them. Many prospectors are down to their last bit of money, having found the trip north much more costly than predicted. The wealthier passengers have no trouble hiring someone to take care of the most mundane tasks.

I wish I could get a letter from you along this never ending river. On one hand I marvel at my surroundings: the towering bluffs, endless forests, primitive Indian villages, desperate men and women. Somehow these experiences seem commonplace, and memories of families, tidy lawns, orchards and cities are foreign. How quickly we assimilate.

Lately I worry that Barrett and I might not agree on how to educate and serve the local natives. The trading post owner in Kaltag, where we stopped a few days ago, reacted strangely when I mentioned who my fiancé is. Is seems that this man winters in Dawson City and knows Barrett. It wasn't what he said, but rather how he said it, but I got the impression he thinks Barrett relies too much on fear to convert the Indians. When Barrett and I spoke last summer about his call to the Yukon Territory, we discussed conversion through love and example. I can't believe he would be so different now.

My friends are treasures; I can't imagine not having them in my life now. Esther Cohen is like a young aunt, who is sure I do not know how to take care of myself! She is a talented seamstress, with an eye for fashion. Molly Green reminds me of an older aunt, who is wise and calm, with a good business sense. Lars and Jimmy are such familiar faces at meal times and strolls along the deck; I get concerned if I don't see them every day. Most of the passengers on board the steamer know each other by name, and I know a few on the barge. We are a tiny community, with a fluctuating location!

Jimmy has come to collect our letters, which he will deliver to the post office. The Captain wants to continue moving up the river, instead of staying in Nulato overnight. The next post office is two weeks away in Ft. Yukon.

Your friend,
Abigail

Rosalie remarked, "I love how Abigail compares her life in Oregon to what she experiences on the river. She doesn't seem to judge people harshly, or form opinions without a great deal of information."

"Yes, Grandma Abigail always saw the best in people she met. To get on her wrong side, you must have been very naughty!" Callie laughed.

Callie poured another round of coffee, and asked Ray to read from the memoir next.

"Captain Jones halted the boat one morning, when two moose were spotted along the shore. By the time the steamer stopped and tied up, the heavy antlered beasts had lumbered into the undergrowth. Three hunters followed their path, and soon a volley of shots was heard, with jubilant 'hurrahs' from our boat. Large haunches were roasted in a pit on the beach, and all passengers welcomed a holiday from the river travel. Sometimes the river's shoreline is strewn with boulders and downed trees, blocking the chance for a bit of exercise along the beach; however this stretch was smooth for as far as we could see. Lars and Jimmy asked if I would like to accompany them for a bit of exploring before our picnic was ready. The day was gloriously warm and sunny; Jimmy collected interesting stones as he ran along in front of us. Lars and I talked earnestly about our dreams. He kept looking so intensely at me I could see my face reflected in his eyes. I remember thinking how different Lars was from Barrett: tall, healthily tanned, and interested in my opinion. Three steamboats passed us on their way up the Yukon; two more going downstream blew their whistles as they almost flew by with the fast current heading to St. Michaels. Lars and I talked about the turns life takes when least expected, speaking mostly about my quick decision to come north and marry. Suddenly Jimmy yelled with fright, and when we reached his side, a horrible sight was exposed on the beach: the body of a man was snagged on a dead tree that stretched across the sand, into the river. Lars waded out and managed to untangle the body, and dragged it onshore. We hurried back to the steamer to inform Captain

Jones; Lars and a crewman took a litter and blanket to fetch the deceased. Lars searched the poor man's pockets for some identification, and found a receipt for passage on a river steamer *Texas* (Kate's boat!) with the name Marco Dante as the passenger. He was buried with a short ceremony just above the waterline, and marked with a wooden cross. Captain Jones reported the death to authorities at the next stop. Kate's boat couldn't be far ahead of us. I wanted so much to sit and laugh with her again; too bad she wasn't here for our picnic. The burial did not dampen spirits at the feast; in fact the evening was quite lively! Lars said something quite thought-provoking to me, when we were back onboard in the late evening. I had said goodnight and turned to proceed down the passageway to my stateroom, when he took my arm gently, and said, 'Abigail, be certain that the life chosen for you is the one you want. There is no shame in changing your mind, before a mistake is made.' Then he stammered, 'I shouldn't have said anything, I'm so sorry.' I didn't know what to say, but I thanked him for his concern, and we parted for the evening. I couldn't get his words out of my head that night. Maybe it was because I had been thinking the same thing.

"By the next morning, sitting on deck in the bright daylight, with the glare of the sun on the river, the situation was clearer in my mind. I convinced myself that the exotic surroundings and proximity to a handsome man had turned my head, and I promised myself I would spend more time with the 'Aunts', and less with Lars. I owed it to Barrett to at least arrive in Dawson City with the idea of marrying him. Foolishly that same evening, my young mind let the romantic sounds of water passing along the steamer's bow, and soft music coming from the barge, reverse my good intentions. After Jimmy slept, Lars and I walked along the decks, forgetting all other people in our lives. Before I slipped back into my stateroom, he pulled me behind some crates of cargo, and kissed me lightly on the lips. Much later, I realized that was the beginning of my point of no return."

"So, I'm still wondering if she married Barrett." Ray said.

Callie remarked, "Abigail was just then discovering that sometimes life is not straightforward, no matter how hard we try."

Ray continued reading the journal aloud, but wondered why Callie didn't answer his question about Barrett.

"Jimmy became very sick, and we were afraid it might be typhoid fever. Several other passengers were down with the same symptoms, which meant our stop in Anvik or Nulato exposed us to the infection. We reached Tanana in the early morning hours of August 16, where St. James Mission operated a real hospital. I was so worried, and Lars was frantic. Jimmy's fever spiked quickly, and aside from trying to cool him down with cold river water, there wasn't much else we could do.

"Lars and I decided to take shifts with Jimmy, afraid to leave him alone for a minute. Thank god for the hospital in Tanana, although medical supplies were in short supply and the nursing staff was small in number. Ft. Gibbon, built downstream earlier that summer to service the planned telegraph line to Nome, supplied a doctor for the hospital. He was quite overwhelmed with so many new patients, but seemed very competent. I had to make a difficult choice a couple of days later, when the *MV Olive May* left Tanana for Dawson City, with the healthy passengers. Jimmy and Lars needed my help; I hoped Barrett would understand. I couldn't even say a proper goodbye to Esther and Molly, for fear of exposing them to the illness. A note from Molly wished us good luck, with assurance we would see each other soon. She also packed a small bag with changes of clothes and personal items I would need while in Tanana. Captain Jones promised to see that the rest of my goods and Barrett's cargo were delivered to him, with my letter of an explanation for the delay. Lars was allowed to sleep by Jimmy's bed, and I had a cot in the nurses' dormitory. The disease soon progressed into incessant diarrhea, and Jimmy had a sunken look around his eyes. Sometimes Lars could get him to suck on a wet cloth to help moisten his mouth, and introduce a small amount of water into his stomach.

"The days and nights rolled together with Lars and me alternating care for the weak and sometimes delirious boy. Lars kept telling me that if anything happened to Jimmy, Myra would never forgive him. I managed to make Lars eat at least once a day, and sleep a little. My duties became less demanding as the days went by, as Jimmy's health miraculously improved. In the evenings, when Jimmy slept, Lars escorted me around the village and hospital grounds. He complimented me often, and declared that my eyes had cast a spell on him. We spent so much time together that some folks in the village assumed Lars and I were married to each other. In truth, I felt myself falling in love with Lars but knew that very soon we would have to part.

"One by one the patients either died, or improved enough to leave the hospital, and after three weeks, that day finally came for Jimmy. On a bright afternoon, we took Jimmy out on the porch, so he could sit in the sun while I cut Lars' straggly hair. It was wonderful hearing Jimmy laugh again, and Lars already looked healthier too. The doctor said that Jimmy could continue the journey to Dawson City in two more days, so we kept watch for a steamer that could make a place for us onboard."

"The episode had taken a toll on Abigail, physically and emotionally," Callie added.

Rosalie wondered aloud, "Did she keep in contact with Lars and Jimmy after they finally reached Dawson City?"

"The next entry is very important on that subject," Callie responded, with a little smile.

"Finally on September 6, passage was arranged for us on the vessel *Laurie Lee*. Oh, what a confused life I had made for myself. Well, I guess I had some help. Over the last few weeks, I had become more and more flattered by Lars' attentions. I knew more about this man than I knew of the man I was to marry and with whom I was supposed to spend the rest of my life.

"The evening before departure, we walked up the hill behind the hospital to escape the tiresome smells of sickness and disinfectant. Lars suddenly faced me and took my hands in his. He said that there was no way he could repay me for my devotion to Jimmy; tears began coursing down his face as if he just realized Jimmy was alright. He let go of my hands and covered his face; Lars had not let himself fall apart while Jimmy was in danger, but the worry seemed to drain from his body through his tears that night. I also became upset and turned to walk a few steps away. Lars caught my hand, and whispered 'Dear Abigail.' He brought me back to his side, drew me so close that I should have pulled away, and he touched my forehead with a feathery kiss. I was shaking with love; I knew it was love. He looked deep into my eyes, and wiped the tears from my cheeks. We stood still for what seemed forever; then he quietly said, 'I apologize.' Confused, I asked, 'Why?' His answer came swift and sweet…a kiss that caused my heart to melt like molten gold, warming every ounce of my being. When we drew apart, he said, 'I've wanted to do that for a very long time. I know you will marry Barrett soon, but remember that more than one man cares for you.' I was stunned and forgot for just a fleeting moment that he belonged to another. Shaking, I boldly said, 'For this one night, I want to forget anyone else exists.' I couldn't look at him when I said this, but he lifted my chin, and when I saw the look on his face, I said, 'I love you, Lars.' It was that simple! I felt this would be my only chance to feel so loved … a very different life was waiting for me at journey's end, but I would have this night as my own."

Rosalie exclaimed, "Uh-oh!"

"Could anyone have predicted such an emotional roller coaster when Abigail left Prineville?" Callie asked.

Ray interjected, "I sort of like Lars, but Abigail hasn't written anything about Lars saying he loves her too."

Ignoring Ray's observation, Callie said, "Abigail and Lars wouldn't see each other again for some time, because an Alaska Commercial Company official demanded passage on the *Laurie Lee*. Lars and Jimmy had to wait for the next steamer; Abigail was determined to stay behind also, but Lars talked her out of it, saying she had to get to Dawson or she would risk having her reputation questioned. Before she boarded the steamer, Jimmy grabbed her around the waist, and cried how he would miss her so much. Abigail hugged the little boy and told him to come see her in Dawson City; she reached out her hand to Lars for a casual handshake. The steamer was packed tightly with passengers, and she had to share a tiny stateroom with three young women who were entertainers, bound for the Klondike."

Callie pulled a letter from the stack that Abigail wrote to Alice, mailed from Ft. Yukon.

September 14, 1898
Ft. Yukon, Alaska Territory

Dear Alice,

Oh, my dear friend, so much has changed about me. I wonder if you would still be my friend if you knew all my secrets. One day, when I see you again, I will unburden my heart and take a chance on your understanding. After a long delay, I am once again traveling up the

Yukon River. I hope a letter from you has overtaken me and is waiting for my arrival in Dawson City. News from home would be a tonic for my mood. Alice, I am struggling with an uncertainty regarding my marriage to Barrett. He and Mother are so positive this is the right thing; yet during these months of travel, my opinion of Barrett is less dear than two months ago. He is a good man, I am sure, but do I admire him enough? He has gone to a great deal of trouble to have me join him in the Klondike, not to mention the expense. Perhaps by the time I arrive in Dawson City, I will know what to do.

The closer we get to the gold fields, the more anxious my fellow passengers become. There is a mood of heightened anxiety with each day that passes. Men are heard exclaiming, "I think we're too late," and "I've gotta get a claim, I'm broke," but mostly "Can't wait to pick up those nuggets off the ground." There's more river traffic now, with boats of all sizes running between Dawson and some of the lower villages. Ft. Yukon buzzes with activity and soldiers patrol the village and river traffic. This settlement is made up of about a dozen cabins, a store, church, and many resident Indians. Their little children are allowed to roam freely, underfoot and half naked, among the crowd. Their mothers are busy slicing huge king salmon down the bellies; with the skin still attached between the two halves, they are hung over poles out of reach from children and dogs. When the salmon is dried, it is stored for human and dog consumption all winter. These northern people have relied on salmon harvests for hundreds, perhaps thousands, of years.

A fight started between two miners outside the trading post just after we tied up; it seems that they are partners on a claim, and had been at odds all year. I could see them rolling around in the mud, and soon some soldiers pulled them apart. Several passengers have gone ashore, including the three young women from my cabin; however,

Ft. Yukon seems awfully rough, so I stayed onboard. The weather is quite blustery, with waves standing on the river, just like we had on the ocean voyage from Seattle. The wind is coming straight down the valley, so our boat will have to fight to make any progress towards Dawson City today.

I so wish I could talk to Mother. She would understand and help me decide what to do about Barrett. In just two weeks we are supposed to be married.

I must get this letter to the captain, who promises to post it for me.

Your friend,

Abigail

VII

. . . .

"THE CLOSER ABIGAIL GOT TO DAWSON CITY, THE more she doubted her reasons for making the journey," Callie said. "There was nothing she could do right then; but Lars' face kept appearing like a reminder of what they shared so many nights ago. Abigail's patience was short in her frustration; some days she felt like screaming at her cabin mates, who often prattled of schemes to make money off the miners who tried to woo them. Abigail met an older couple from Boise who were going to open their boot shop in the booming city. Mr. and Mrs. Robertson and Abigail enjoyed sitting alongside the rail on pleasant days, while he read, and the women sewed. Abigail embroidered flowers on handkerchiefs Emily had hemmed for her. Somehow it helped her feel closer to home."

"Can you imagine having to wait months to hear from friends and family?" Rosalie asked no one in particular.

Callie nodded, and asked Rosalie to read the next part.

"We came upon an amazing sight right after we left Ft. Yukon; we spied small boats tied up to crumbling bluffs, with men chipping away at things embedded in the mud. The captain approached the bluffs, and hailed a boat over to our side. I was surprised to see that in the bottom of the boat were several white logs, which weren't logs at all. They were bones and tusks of giant mastodons which roamed this area thousands of years ago. The men harvesting the ivory tusks were just as excited about their discovery as the gold seekers onboard our steamer were about finding their glittering fortunes in the streams of the Klondike.

"Our next stop was Circle City, which had its own gold rush a few years ago; now most of the town had relocated to diggings nearer Dawson. It was strange to see the forests cut down far up the river banks, from years of stoking the boilers on hundreds of steamers plying the Yukon. The village of Eagle boasted a trading post, and had a large Indian population. I purchased a pair of beaded leather moccasins from an old woman sitting on a log near the trading post. She was terribly wrinkled and thin, and smiled a mostly toothless grin when I stopped to examine her handiwork. My boot maker friends, the Robertsons, approved the workmanship and said that the moccasin maker was toothless because she chewed hides to make them velvety soft for her use.

"The Forty Mile River joins the Yukon near the Canadian border; a village at this junction also enjoyed an earlier gold rush, but was ghostly quiet, with abandoned cabins up and down the river. Our boat began experiencing engine problems so we tied up to some old stumps while the engineer tried to diagnose the loss of power. He finally declared we could proceed, but at a slower speed.

"The Captain announced we would arrive in Dawson City about noon the next day, and suddenly I rather dreaded completing the journey. After travelling over 6,000 miles from my home in Oregon, I was nothing like the girl of four months ago. Forging ahead with my wedding plans, I bathed and washed my hair, and smoothed the wrinkles from a new dress in my trunk. The bonnet Molly and Esther fashioned for me was ready to wear atop a fashionable pouf one of my young cabin mates, Jennie, offered to arrange the next morning. I had come to appreciate those gay young women for their kindnesses, after learning more about their reasons for coming north. I couldn't judge them harshly, because wasn't I making a bargain to find a better life? I remembered what a thoughtful person Kate was, and how I wanted to see her again, no matter what she did for a living. By the time I reached Dawson, my decision had been made about marrying Barrett; it was the best for all of us if I married him right away. Even if Lars never faded from my dreams, I could make certain Barrett never knew of it."

"Well, she finally arrived in Dawson!" Callie exclaimed. "Even though Abigail thought the Yukon River trip was an adventure, it had only just begun."

"Now you've done it … we just want to keep hearing more and more, but it's late," Rosalie said.

Ray explained that they were meeting a book collector in Bend for dinner at their hotel, and should get on the road.

Callie said, "I go to bed with the chickens nowadays, but why don't you come back in the morning? I'm up by 5:00."

Rosalie quickly accepted the invitation, but confirmed they'd be there about 8:00 a.m. Wild horses couldn't keep her from coming back to hear more of Abigail's story.

Callie had coffee and homemade donuts waiting when Rosalie and Ray arrived just before 8:00 the next morning. When asked how their evening had been, Rosalie explained that the collector in Bend specialized in classical rare editions, and had seen a book he liked in their online catalog. The third edition of Mary Shelley's *Frankenstein* printed in 1831, bound in red morocco leather was nothing short of magnificent, and he had to have it. The gentleman had planned to drive to Portland in a few days to pick it up, but the timing for their trip to Callie's was perfect.

As soon as Callie had everyone settled with their plates and mugs, she picked up Abigail's memoir. Before she began reading, Callie confided, "Grandma Abigail often said her first months in Dawson were like being in a fog that swept in and out, never predictable."

"Our overloaded, belching steamboat made landing on October 1, 1898 in Dawson City, Klondike District, Yukon Territory, Canada. Some prospectors came upstream on the Yukon River as we did, and others floated downstream from Lake Bennett after trekking over the pass from Dyea or Skagway. The town's only dock was already packed with boats of all sizes and for a mile up and down the river dozens of other crafts like ours were tethered to the shore. The captain pulled the *Laurie Lee* alongside the river bank and the crew tossed out a gangplank to disgorge her passengers. There was so much noise on board with folks trying to keep sight of their baggage, party members, or family, that I almost missed hearing my name being shouted; Barrett was waving madly, trying to get my attention. Such a feeling of relief engulfed me from head to toe, and soon he scooped me from the gangplank, and waded through the deep mud along the beach. Barrett had never allowed himself to publically display affections in Oregon, but here on the banks of the Yukon River, he kissed me soundly on the lips while clutching me close. He said 'I got the cargo and your big trunks from the *Olive May* three weeks ago, and your friends told me about your delay in Tanana, but we can talk about that later.' The crush of a human tide soon pushed us up the beach to a rutted track where a small wagon and horse were tended by a young Indian man. I told Barrett where he would find my bag, and he said, 'Abigail, this is Moses. He works for me and will stay with you while I go back.' Moses spoke English very well, and later I learned he had been educated at an Indian school in Oregon. As soon as Barrett returned, we started off through the crowd. The sheer number of men milling around the streets quickly overwhelmed me; coming from months of limited contact with people, to seeing thousands all at once, made me burrow into Barrett's shoulder. Gold seekers, merchants, shabby panhandlers, brightly dressed women, Indians… what a wild place it was.

The wagon wound its way up a hill until we were beyond most of the other cabins scattered along the flatland by the river. I questioned Barrett, remembering his letter said we had a cabin next to the church. He answered, not looking at me, that he was no longer pastor. I must have exclaimed something, because he boldly announced that I shouldn't worry, since he had filed a claim eighteen miles up the Klondike River. Within just one hour, half of the reason I came to Dawson was gone: no church for Barrett, no school for me. Barrett and Moses had built another cabin, and as we approached the location, I had to admit I liked being away from the chaos of town. I realized he was worried about my comfort here, because Barrett proudly said he designed a double-walled cabin, with a full 12 inches of moss and dirt between the two walls to insulate it against the cold. The outside walls were constructed with full round logs, and the inside layer was made with small split logs with the flat side facing inward. The floor was planked and covered with animal skins and he had installed a cast iron stove, which served for cooking and heating the living area. Another smaller stove sat in the bedroom for use in the winter. Our furniture was rustic, with one exception: a claw foot oak table, spread with a silk fringed shawl, made the hastily built cabin seem more of a permanent home.

Barrett arranged for a judge to marry us in his office that very afternoon. I was already dressed in my wedding clothes, so after freshening up, we drove back down the hill. A few people on the streets nodded to Barrett as we passed, however some seemed to avoid contact. The judge was pleasant, and his wife served as our witness. I hardly remembered the words spoken, but I felt that Barrett was sincere in his vows. The ring he chose to seal our marriage was a wide gold band, engraved inside with our names. Afterward, my new husband escorted me along the planked sidewalk to a photographer's office, where we posed for our wedding portrait. A friend of Barrett's, Tom Doaks, caught up with us on the street, and insisted that he take us to dinner. Barrett swept me up in his arms and carried me across the quagmire that passed for a street, to the Astoria Restaurant. I never forgot that meal; we ate veal prepared in a luscious sauce, and fresh vegetables from the cook's own greenhouse. I listened to the men talking about the gold strikes, and I detected a glint in Barrett's eyes that reminded me of the men onboard our steamer, who were half-crazed to find gold. Back at our cabin we talked more about the mine, but Barrett said nothing about leaving the church. When it finally came time to go to bed, I was left alone in the bedroom where I washed and put on my new batiste gown. Barrett was very gentle, and explained that it would be over quickly, so I should not be afraid. Later, he went to sleep, and I lay still, wondering where my life was headed.

"The next morning when I opened my eyes, Barrett was gone. In the main room the young woman hired by my husband was humming as she kneaded dough. I remembered her name was Etta, so I introduced myself, and asked if she knew where Mr. Rogers had gone. Etta replied in passable English that he and Moses had gone to the claim, and would be back in about a week. Well, it wasn't exactly the kind of honeymoon I had expected. The crates of food that arrived on the *Olive May* earlier had been unpacked and stored, but I had three trunks filled with all kinds of household goods to sort. Over the next two days, Etta and I hung curtains sewn from fabric given me by the Aunts; washed, ironed, brushed and aired all my clothing; unpacked linens and kitchen ware. The curtains certainly made the rooms homier, although we didn't really have windows. Small openings in two walls were simply covered with a thin animal skin which had been greased, but it did allow in enough light to keep the cabin from feeling like a cave. I learned later that in the winter, with so little daylight anyway, the windows were covered with anything to keep out the cold.

"Not one inch of wall, floor, or ceiling space was wasted. The main room was about twelve feet wide and fourteen feet long, and was furnished with the stove in the middle of the room, the table, two chairs, a narrow cot, and a bench which held a wash basin. Underneath the bench were shelves holding pots and mismatched dishes. In several places along the cabin walls, shelves held cans and sacks of food. A plainly framed mirror hung near the door, and several boxes of heavy clothing, boots, and tools were stored under the cot. A door in the room's back wall led to the tiny bedroom; it was twelve feet wide, like the main room, but only deep enough for a narrow space on each side of the bed. A sturdy bureau took up part of a side wall, and pegs for clothes were behind the door. The tiny stove used during the coldest nights occupied a spot near the back wall, with a sheet of iron between it and the logs. The ceilings in both rooms were festooned with sacks of clothes and dried foods and a shotgun dangled within easy reach near the bedroom door. A queer log box, raised on ten-foot stilts, stood near the cabin; in fact similar structures accompanied many other cabins around the hills. I learned this 'cache' would hold frozen meat during the winters, safely out of reach from dogs and other animals.

"Etta was very quiet, but efficient in whatever chore she undertook. When I asked how long she had kept house for Barrett, she replied it was about three months. Barrett told me that most of her family had been moved into the Provincial preserve set aside for the

Han Indians, mostly to get them out of the way of the tide of men who wanted to want to prospect without confronting scattered Indian families in the hills. Since the weather was cooler, and mosquitoes were less of a problem, some evenings Etta and I sat outside on a well-placed bench, from where we could watch the river traffic on the Yukon. The scene from that distance was peaceful and picturesque, without the filth and noise one encountered in town. Etta told me that the town's location, where the Yukon and Klondike Rivers merge, was an Indian hunting camp before gold was discovered. White men had been coming up the great river for decades; but nothing like this had ever been seen before.

"One morning I heard a wagon pull up outside, and thought Barrett might be back. When I opened the door, there was Kate, laughing and tightly hugging me! I was never so happy to see a person in all my life! She had been in Dawson about a month; I told her about my marriage, which caused her forehead to wrinkle. When Kate heard that Barrett was gone, she promptly told me to get dressed for a trip to town. What a time we had! She took me to the Aunts new store, a block off Front Street. Esther and Molly were ecstatic that I had finally arrived safely in Dawson. Their business was booming already, with orders and fittings for ladies of Dawson society, plus Kate's theater friends. The inventory that came on the steamer with them was dwindling; however, they learned that orders for more supplies could be brought in by sledge from Skagway during the winter, now that there was a new road that bypassed Chilkoot Pass. I was so happy for their success and purchased some wool yarn for stockings, since I had to find something to keep myself busy while Barrett was at the mine. I didn't yet know what my place would be in the social life of Dawson City, since I had depended on having a built-in circle of friends through the church and school.

"Kate took me back to the cabin, and over another cup of tea she said she had heard about Barrett being asked to leave his church. When she saw the look on my face, and realized that I didn't know that little detail, Kate quickly said 'no matter' and I gladly accepted a change of subject. Later I decided that detail was the reason some people we met on the street the day I arrived were less than friendly. When she asked where Lars and Jimmy were, I told her about our scare in Tanana, and circumstances which put them on a later boat. But I didn't share more than that. I told her about the body of Marco Dante we found, which appeared to have fallen from the *Texas*. She remembered him as an occasional actor, and said she would tell his brother he had been found. Too soon, Kate had to leave to dress for her evening performances, but we made plans to meet again. Etta had been sitting by the stove, stirring vegetables into a pot of soup for our supper. She helped Kate put the long cloak over her fancy dress, and then went to the door to watch the beautiful young woman lift her skirts and climb into the wagon. Turning around, Etta eyed me, and asked, 'that one, she is your friend?' When I said yes, she responded, 'I think Mr. Rogers would not like that.' For a moment I panicked, but somehow forced myself to smile and said, "Well, then we just won't tell Mr. Rogers, will we?" With a twinkle in her eyes, she slowly put a finger up to her lips, which made me giggle.

"When Barrett had been gone ten days, I wondered why I was even in Dawson City. Without Esther Cohen, Molly Green and Kate Rockwell, I couldn't have faced the coming winter. Etta seemed to keep a vigil for Barrett's return.

"I wondered and worried where Lars and Jimmy were."

"Wow," Rosalie said, shaking her head, when Callie laid the journal on her lap. "I can understand why she wondered about her decision to come north."

"She told me that at that time she thought of getting on a steamer, going back down river. Ice was already forming along shorelines on some stretches of the Yukon, so time was limited for an escape." Callie said.

Ray asked, "Why didn't she?"

"Abigail had to see Lars again, and she knew he could find her if she stayed in Dawson," Callie explained.

"Ooohhhh, I should have realized," said Rosalie.

Callie retrieved an envelope from the end table, and reminded them that Abigail was still alone with Etta.

October 12, 1898
Dawson City, Yukon Territory

Dear Alice,

What a wonderful surprise! Yesterday I decided to walk down the hill to Dawson City's Post Office. Etta, my housekeeper, said I could not go alone and accompanied me along the icy road into town. A long line of men and a few women stretched from the log cabin's door into the frozen, rutted street; Etta rolled her eyes when we got within hearing distance of the rough miners. She said, "Miss Abby, You go see Miss Green, I wait in line." I didn't correct her abbreviation of my name; my thought was that if it made her more comfortable, it was acceptable. There was some doubt whether the postmaster would give her any mail addressed to me or Barrett, so I stayed. After just a few minutes, a familiar voice called my name; Barrett's friend, Tom Doaks, who had provided our wedding dinner, motioned me to where he stood just outside the post office's door. He graciously announced, "These gentlemen won't mind a bit if you cut in line, Mrs. Rogers," and I turned to see a dozen of the nearest men in line remove their caps or nod in agreement. Mr. Doaks said he knew Barrett was still at the mine; in fact he had seen my husband just two days ago. He asked if there were something he could do for me while in town; I replied that yes, there was: I needed to hire someone to haul water to our barrel in the cabin two times a week. So far, Etta has been asking various teamsters to bring us a few buckets, but they weren't dependable long term. Mr. Doaks said he would see to it, not to worry. Anyway, once I appeared before the postmaster and stated my name, he looked in the "R" box, and found nothing for me. Disappointed of course, I suddenly remembered to have him look at mail for the First Methodist Church, and he discovered two letters!

I am blathering nonsense to you! What I want to say is I can't tell you what your letter means to me! By now you have received more of my letters to you, posted along the Yukon River.

Alice, I have been married twelve days, and haven't seen my husband since the first night. He is no longer a church pastor; I do not know the reasons for that. He is now working a claim somewhere up the Klondike River about eighteen miles from Dawson City. We have a cabin on the edge of town where my housekeeper Etta keeps me company. My friends, Esther Cohen and Molly Green (the "Aunts"), have a wonderful shop of ladies' fashions near Front Street, and I visit with them as often as possible. Kate, who is performing at the Orpheum Theater, makes me laugh when she visits me at home or at the Aunts' shop. An older couple, Mr. and Mrs. Robertson from Boise, whom I met on the steamer from Tanana, have opened their boot shop and are so busy they've had to hire two men to help. The town is so filled with a distortion of characters that it is comforting to see a familiar, friendly face! There is no word from Lars and Jimmy Jensen, who were on a steamer somewhere behind me. The river will be frozen solid within a month, maybe sooner; nights already are quite cold. There isn't a lot of snow yet, but the old timers say we are due for it very soon. This morning the man who delivers water arrived with a wagon full of firewood and several small kegs of water. Mr. Johnson and his brother transferred the water into our barrel in the kitchen area, and stacked the wood beside the cabin. He said the bill was paid and more will be delivered when he sees I need it. I will have to thank Mr. Doaks with a home cooked meal next time we meet.

As much as I thought I knew about the Yukon Territory, gleaning information from all those I met on the trip, I never dreamed how life here would be so fragile. A journey over mountain passes and glaciers take the lives of many gold seekers; and for those who arrive with empty pockets, food becomes the real treasure. A can of gold nuggets will disappear in one wrong bet at the poker table; yet, it's not uncommon to hear a destitute miner in the morning is wealthy by evening. Actresses (and saloon dancers) collect nuggets thrown at their feet each night, and quickly spend them on Paris gowns and hats. At the same time, miners' wives take in laundry and boarders, just to put food on the table until the spring thaw when gold can be washed out of the diggings.

The news of your baby expected in the spring is wonderful. You sound so happy in Cross Hollows, decorating your new house. I hope to see it for myself next year. I also received a letter from Mother yesterday; her burden seems to get heavier each year. My stepfather is suffering with lung fever and is unable to work; Emily is not in school this term, since she has to help with the house chores, while Mother does the best she can with the livestock. Once Barrett begins to make money from his claim, I want to hire a farmhand to work for her. It appears that Barrett's family no longer provides him with a stipend for living expenses; however, I arrived in Dawson with a little money left from the travel funds Barrett provided. We also have one thousand pounds of dried and canned foodstuff Barrett had shipped up this summer; so with a roof, food and a way to keep warm, I will fare well this winter even if Barrett stays at the claim.

Mr. Doaks explained that during the winter, prospectors build small fires in the bottom of their diggings, to thaw a few inches at a time of the granite-hard frozen gravel. Visible nuggets can be picked out of the muck, but most of the gravel is simply brought to the surface in buckets, thrown on an accumulating pile, where it refreezes until the spring thaw. As soon as water flows through the flumes, the gravel can be washed and the gold is then collected. It sounds simple, but the work must be agonizing with the temperatures dipping near forty below zero for weeks at a time. Barrett and Moses have a tiny cabin at the claim, so at least they are safe and warm.

I wish I could say I am blissfully happy to be Barrett's wife, but right now I don't even feel married. Please continue to write. I am told that mail will come in and out of Dawson City about once a month this winter, through Skagway over the snowy trails and frozen rivers.

The Aunts told me they saw Lars and Jimmy on the street; they were headed up El Dorado Creek for the winter. He knows I am married now.

Your Dawson friend,

Abigail

When Callie's phone rang, Rosalie and Ray jumped; they had been mesmerized by Abigail's description of her surroundings, and what she faced that winter. Callie walked into her kitchen with the phone, saying, "Uh-huh, uh-huh, good….ok, see you then. Bye, honey."

"That was my daughter; she's driving down today and will be here about supper time. I'm so glad you'll get to meet her," Callie said.

"I would love that," Rosalie said.

"Rosalie, I'll pour another round of coffee; then would you like to read from the memoir for awhile?" Callie asked.

"Of course I will!"

"By December 1st, I had spent six weeks in my own personal hell. Etta made sure I ate and bathed, but I'm certain I gave her no good reason to stay with me.

"Barrett worked at the mine about three weeks, before he and Moses got back to Dawson. They were very excited to show me the contents of a fist-sized canvas bag, and the gold nuggets Barrett poured onto the table ranged in size from a pea to a peach pit. He hugged me close and twirled me off my feet, while Etta and Moses stood aside, giggling at our foolishness. After a hasty meal, Moses said he wanted to clean up at the bath house used by the Indian men on the other end of town, and would see us in a couple of days. Etta heated water for Barrett's bath in the galvanized tub in our bedroom, and then said she would like to be gone a few days to her sister's house. Our second night as husband and wife was sweet as could be, and we talked about our plans for the future. The mine, which he named the Black Dog, didn't seem to be overly rich, but hopefully a steady producer. He laughingly told me he was no longer considered a Cheechako or tenderfoot; his last winter in Dawson had earned his place as a Sourdough. Barrett agreed that I should send Mother some money to help with the ranch, and that endeared him to me even more.

"Next morning Barrett's mass of red hair made me laugh at its unruliness, so I sat him on one of our stools to trim the straggly strands. I don't believe he had taken his hat off the whole time at the claim and didn't realize how long it was. Barrett wanted to buy me a locket, so I saved a curl of his hair for it. We bundled up and walked to the Aunts' shop on Main Street, now called Maison de Mode, or House of Fashion. I also introduced him to the Robertsons, and he introduced me to the bank manager. The owner of Rothstein Jewelers had the perfect locket for me: heart-shaped, sterling silver filigree design on a long, braided silver chain. We stopped by the photographer's shop to retrieve our wedding portrait. I was so happy that day.

"That evening, I prepared a rich oyster stew from our cache of canned meats. We heard a commotion outside so Barrett opened the door, and yelled for me to see the horrific scene in town. By the time I reached the door, Barrett was pulling on his boots and coat. Several buildings were blazing like hell itself, with explosions sending debris and more flames onto neighboring buildings. Even from our location up on the hill above town, I could hear the crowd yelling, along with the whooshing of the firestorm. Barrett told me to stay at the cabin where I'd be safe, and kissed me on the forehead.

"That was the last time I saw him.

"The fire jumped, building by building, finally reaching the hospital. Barrett was seen charging inside to save patients who were trapped. They never made it out; the roof crashed onto the second floor, which in turn brought down the whole structure. Mr. Doaks came to tell me the next morning, with Moses at his side. I don't remember much about the next week. I know Etta dressed and fed me and Esther and Molly came every day; Kate spent every morning at the cabin until I assured her that Etta and I would be fine. My young companion also grieved over Barrett's death, probably because she was aware how difficult life will be for us now. I hardly knew Barrett, but I had just begun to accept that we might have a good life together. We buried his remains in the small church cemetery, and I now have to inform his family in Oregon. The destroyed buildings in Dawson City are being quickly rebuilt, several bigger and better. Thank goodness the Maison de Mode was spared.

"The prospect of having to stay in Dawson by myself this winter petrified me; suddenly everything and everybody seems foreign and frightening. Etta never considered moving back with her people, which means a lot to me. A few more cabins have been built on my hill, but only men come and go. Sometimes just standing in the doorway, looking over the river valley, makes me tremble. All I have left of Barrett is our wedding portrait, ring, and a curl of his hair in my locket. I feel so small in this enormous land, and nothing like the girl who left Oregon six months ago. Nevertheless, I will have my baby in early summer, and return home on one of the first steamers leaving Dawson."

"Oh, no! She's pregnant!" Rosalie exclaimed, sitting straight up in her chair.

"That happens," quipped Ray, as he lifted one eyebrow.

"You know what I mean. She is alone…sort of, and sad," said Rosalie. "I'll bet she was scared out of her wits."

Callie nodded, "Abigail was afraid, but she was made from pioneer stock that wasn't prone to falling apart. Go ahead Rosalie, read on!"

VIII

. . . .

"THE DAYS BECAME BITTERLY COLD IN JANUARY, AND the nights were colder; but of course, it was hard to tell night from day right then. The thermometer only recorded down to forty below zero. Etta kept a bottle of oil sludge hanging from a post outside; she claimed that when the contents became slushy, it was forty below, but when the sludge froze, the temperature was at least fifty below zero. I had to be so careful when walking outside. I soon learned why Barrett told me to buy a parka with a hood that pulled up so hardly any of my face showed. I'd heard of several men who had frozen their cheeks, noses or lips after just a few minutes of exposure; worse was when a man froze his lungs.

"For the first time in my life I saw the northern lights in all their glory! One evening when Etta and I left the Aunts', a rippling band of green and purple swished across the sky, and I very nearly thought I felt, more than heard, a crackling sensation. Etta laughed and said I was imagining things, but I'd heard that Indians believed the lights were the souls of their ancestors. We watched the display of lights change from purple to green to pink, and in different shapes of curtain-like waves that danced around the sky. If it hadn't been so cold, I would've spent every evening that winter outside, waiting for the lights to appear.

"Almost every day I walked down to Maison de Mode where

Molly and Esther patiently taught me how to sew the finer fabrics used in Kate's costumes. I told my friends about the baby, so they tended to coddle me too much. On Sundays Kate usually swept in with a basket of sweets from the new French Bakery, and told stories she heard from prospectors, about their hard luck, or found fortunes. One day when I entered the bakery, the banker's wife Mrs. Holder, turned her back on me when I nodded a greeting. I couldn't understand why some of Dawson's society treated me so rudely. Just a handful of people from Barrett's former church came to express condolences for his death; for many others, it was like they never knew him. At the time I thought that Tom Doaks must know why, but he revealed nothing. Moses was still working the claim, and he stayed up there to keep an eye on things. Tom helped me hire a lawyer to register the Black Dog Mine in my name, using the certificate of marriage as proof of my ownership.

"Etta was an angel; she kept the cabin warm, and when I taught her some new recipes, she worked hard to make me fatter with her stews and pies. I found out that her father was a white man who came to the Yukon looking for gold in the Forty Mile district eighteen years ago. During the winter I discovered that Etta was expecting a child. When I asked if she had a husband, Etta just shrugged. When I asked if Moses were the father, she just said 'Miss Abby!' and shook her head. I suspected she caught some prospector's eye before I came. Those indigenous girls continued to be used by the white men, intruders into a country that belonged to the 'first nation.' Once proud hunters, the Indian men around the gold fields were often seen drunk with whiskey, cheated out of their possessions, and many had become dependent on white man's food. When Moses came to town for supplies, he slept on a pallet in front of the stove. During suppers I asked him to share stories with us about his ancestors; his opinion was that most of their lives changed for the worst with the arrival of the Russians, the first white men they saw. Etta always remained silent, but since her white father abandoned the family, I suspected she shared the same opinion as Moses. In his case, a missionary arranged for his schooling 'outside' (a term used for anywhere besides the North.) Moses was employed by the church, but left when Barrett did, to join him in working the claim. Although I became owner of the mine, Moses still got half the gold as long as he worked there. He helped me make good decisions about money and investments in the mine. On his advice, I sold the horse and wagon, since it was easy to arrange delivery of supplies to the mine with Tom. I didn't want to pay someone to stable the horse for us in town; walking to the shops was easy, and in a pinch, I could use Molly's buggy.

"Etta insisted on doing all the housework, which I appreciated, but I finally convinced her I had to have something to do. We agreed I would take over baking the bread for us and the Aunts. After Barrett died, I asked Etta how much he paid her a week; she just shrugged, so I put ten dollars in a jar on the kitchen shelf every Saturday.

"Kate spent one or two mornings a week at the cabin, and the subject most on her mind was a man named Alexander Pantages. I had seen him at a distance, and didn't find him particularly attractive, but Kate believed she had found love at last. I was quite aware of Kate's risqué reputation, since the costumes made for her were quite immodest, with bare shoulders and raised hemlines. She sang and danced, and Molly said, teased men to think she might favor them with more attention. Knowing all this, we still liked Kate, who was quick to help in a crisis and always brought the sun into a room. She insisted on being discreet for the sake of our reputations, and slipped into Maison de Mode unseen. Kate always arrived at my cabin door wrapped in an old hooded coat. Etta pretended she didn't listen to our gossip, but sometimes we heard her giggling behind her dish-towel, and we all three would end up laughing. I think our little cabin represented home and family to Kate, and we were like sisters who accepted each other's faults.

For all my talk, at night when I was no longer engaged with friends or household activities, I slipped into another domain: fear and doubt. Some nights, sleep came only after I'd exhausted myself with tears over being so far from my family, and unsure of what to do.

January 10, 1899

Dear Alice,

My dear friend, I have waited these three months before writing, because the news is difficult to share.

My husband of a month was killed in a fire that swept through Dawson City. Alice, I have to say that I hardly knew Barrett, but still I was devastated when he died and couldn't bring myself to write you until now. There are mysteries surrounding his life here which I may never understand. One of his friends, Tom Doaks, helped me record the cabin deed and gold mine in my name, as Barrett's survivor, and makes certain that I have plenty of firewood and supplies.

I will have a baby in early summer. Yes, it is true. After the baby is born, we will take a boat back down the Yukon River, and return home by mid-August. Barrett's gold claim, the Black Dog Mine, continues to produce a supply of nuggets, but we have to wait until the gravel can be washed after the spring thaw to know the full value of the diggings. Dawson is a town that never sleeps, and it is unbelievable that crime is limited to a few minor incidents. The Canadian Royal Mounted Police make sure the law is upheld here, which I am told is much better than towns in Alaska Territory. I am surrounded by good friends: Etta, Molly and Esther, Kate, Tom Doaks and the Robertsons. The only ones missing are Lars and Jimmy. To help pass the time during these dark, winter days, I am learning to sew beautiful dresses at Maison de Mode. Do not worry about me!

Your friend,

Abigail

"One morning a note came from the Aunts that I should come to the shop right away; of course I anticipated that one of them was sick. I hurried as fast as I dared in the terribly cold weather, with a thick wool scarf wrapped across my face to warm the air before it was sucked into my lungs. In no way was I prepared for the heart stopping scene in the Aunts' upstairs sitting room. Lars looked up as I burst in the door, from where he was hovered over Jimmy. We briefly acknowledged each other, but turned quickly to the boy. Jimmy was pale and listless, but recognized my voice and opened his eyes. He looked so small beneath the layers of quilts and furs Esther kept tucked around him. Lars told us they ran out of provisions; he had gone up and down the creek, asking other miners if they had anything to spare, but everyone was hard up for food. Finally, they started for Dawson, but Jimmy gave out after a few miles; Lars carried him until he found a sled to borrow and arrived at the Aunts only to collapse on the steps.

"I spooned hot soup slowly into Jimmy, and soon he smiled and snuggled deeper into the quilts to sleep. Lars finally ate and I helped pull off his boots. He asked for some warm water to wash his face and hands, and Molly insisted they heat water for a bath which would help him relax and sleep better. Lars told me he spent a few days around Dawson after they docked, and found it true that the claims near town were already taken. He said he wondered if I had arrived alright, and even walked past the church. He asked a passerby about Reverend Rogers, and was told he and his new wife now lived at the other end of Dawson. Lars said when he finally talked to Esther he knew we all were safe; they moved on to work a claim for one of the early prospectors. Supplies were supposed to be delivered every two weeks, but something happened to the owner about the time the weather turned so bitter. When Lars needed help, he knew he could count on the Aunts, and he knew where they were. I was so happy to see him sitting before me, especially since we knew Jimmy would recover after some food and rest. Lars blamed himself for almost killing his son, and regretted bringing him to the Klondike.

"Lars quietly told me he couldn't leave Jimmy with 'those two women.' I didn't know what to say. Lars said he had tried to protect Jimmy from his wife's and sister-in-law selfish behavior, but as the boy grew older he understood the family strife. According to Lars, Myra would not give him a divorce. I wanted to take Lars in my arms, and tell him everything would be better, but that was impossible. Etta came to fetch me, so I wouldn't be walking up the hill alone in the early darkness, and I told everyone I would come back the next day. When I was ready to slip out the door, Lars took my arm and softly whispered, 'Thank you for coming. I have no right to want to see you, but it means a lot to Jimmy. Perhaps your husband would like to come too.' He didn't know Barrett was dead. I saw Etta out of the corner of my eye crook her head towards me; I nudged her ahead of me out into the frigid night. I knew that by morning, Lars would know everything about my marriage and baby."

"So Lars was stuck with a wife he really didn't love, but couldn't end the marriage," Rosalie said.

Ray added, "Too bad, since Barrett is out of the picture. She could use a husband about now, with a baby on the way."

Callie said, "Grandma Abigail told me that up until she saw Lars, she hadn't thought much beyond leaving on a steamer with her baby in the summer. Now that he was back, she was faced with having to decide what to do, because it would affect more people than just herself. Etta had asked why Abigail didn't explain that Barrett was dead. She said the horror of the events still haunted her, and she knew the Aunts would tell him. Abigail was already trying to justify why she had not yet heard back from Barrett's family after writing them of his death. She had chosen not to tell them about the baby just yet, but if they wanted to be part of the child's life, she should move back to Oregon as soon as possible. Abigail writes next about meeting with Lars the next day."

"Lars appeared at my cabin door the next morning. He held my hands, and said 'Molly and Esther told me about your husband's death. I'm really sorry.' He asked if I knew why Barrett was asked to leave the church; I told him I hadn't been able to find out, and maybe I didn't want to know anyway. We sat for a long time, each speaking of life's complications and uncertainties. I asked, 'Did the Aunts tell you about the baby?' He looked down at his hands like they held the right thing to say. I told him that Barrett's family didn't know about the baby. I planned to tell them after they'd had time to accept his death. There had been some friction between Barrett and his parents, so I was waiting for a reply to the letter I sent in November. Lars just nodded in agreement; the atmosphere in the cabin was electric with unspoken words. I wanted Lars to hold me in his arms, but I knew what would happen if I gave in to more than a chaste touch of hands. Etta had slipped out on an errand, so we were alone in the cabin. I finally told Lars he should go, but before he left, he said, 'You know that you can always count on me, Abigail.'

"Later that day, I returned to the shop to see how Jimmy was feeling. Lars had found out that the man who owned the mine where he was employed died, and his son didn't know about provisioning the far flung claims. Once the situation at the mine was corrected, Lars wanted to finish out the season through the clean up and collect his share of the gold. The Aunts presented Lars with an idea: Jimmy could stay with them while Lars was at the claim, so he could attend the new school in Dawson City. While all the planning was underway, Kate burst through the back door, and gave Jimmy a bear hug. She bubbled with excitement that Lars and Jimmy were safe, and wholeheartedly approved the new plan. Kate pressed several gold nuggets into Lars' palm, with kindly instructions to buy Jimmy new clothes for school, and supply his own larder with food so he wouldn't have to depend solely on the mine owner. He clasped her hands and insisted it was just a loan until spring.

"Tom had dropped off a moose's hindquarter at my cabin earlier in the week, and Etta arrived at the Aunts with a large kettle of pot roast and hot sourdough buns. Dehydrated onions, canned turnips and carrots floated in the gravy with an aroma that threatened to drive everyone in the room mad. Jimmy had first chance at the sumptuous meal, and soon we all were sopping gravy and moaning over the tender chunks of meat. Just as our meal was finished, Tom knocked at the door. He had purchased twenty cases of eggs that came by sled from Skagway, packed in straw to keep from freezing. The Aunts and I each bought a case, and talked him into eating from the kettle and staying for fresh raisin pie Esther made. The remaining eggs were delivered to several restaurants and a few families, after Tom took Etta and I home.

"I had a good feeling that night, about all my friends being together again. I felt that as a group we could survive whatever fell across our paths. I heard Etta humming in the kitchen, which echoed my own thoughts.

Ray interrupted, "This fellow, Tom, seemed to be pretty important to those ladies. He was the go-to guy."

Callie puffed a little laugh, "Yes, they were lucky to have Tom because he had been in the Klondike District about two years, and knew all about getting what a person needed."

"In March I talked Moses into finding someone who could carry me by dog sled to the mine. Tom Doaks was away up-river, so Moses said he would ask around. We'd had a break in the weather, and although the snow was deep and heavy, at least the temperatures had risen.

"Moses showed up with a local freighter, who drove a 10-dog team. My partner must have told him about my condition, because he seemed to be careful and drove much slower than when I've seen these sleds bolting down Front Street or on the frozen river. Moses ran alongside the sled, and the driver perched on the back runners or ran, yelling instructions to the lead dogs. The claim cabin was neat as a pin and as cold as a glacier; however, Moses soon had a fire blazing in the stove, and brewed a pot of coffee. After a rest and warm-up, he helped me walk around the mine's edge, and explained how he removed the gravel when it was thawed by burning chunks of wood in the bottom. Within a few minutes of being dumped on the growing pile at the top, the dirt and gravel froze solid until summer. If Moses saw nuggets in the shovelful, he took it into the cabin and washed the mud in a bucket of water. I think I had a clearer understanding of how gold mining got under the skin of a prospector. We unloaded Moses' supplies, ate some bread and canned beef, before the driver once more covered me with heavy robes, and we struck out for home. When we reached The Forks, the driver asked if I wanted to stop at the roadhouse, but I was anxious to get home. Just as Barrett had described in his letter, moonlit nights are actually brighter than the dark winter days, so we were comfortable mushing along the trail. Soon, the lights of Dawson loomed ahead.

"There was so much to learn about my young companion, Etta, and one night she proved that she was exceedingly brave! The two of us spent half an hour in the late evening bundled up, watching the northern lights flash and weave across a starry sky. Adding to the mystical impression, we heard a faint howl from the hills above our cabin, which was answered from one and then another location in the forest. It seemed the howls gradually merged into one place, and echoed closer and closer, until I sighted the wolves' shadowy forms darting in and out of the tree line, and onto the snow drifts covering the field behind the cabin. Tom had warned us that wolves had been coming closer to town, looking for food, since game was in short supply. It seemed wise to hurry inside, and Etta bolted the door. We heard the sound of many feet running around and around the cabin, and then one wolf threw himself against the door. What sounded like dozens of claws tore at the door frame. By this time, Etta had snagged Barrett's shotgun from the rafter and quickly dropped a shell into each chamber. Suddenly, I saw the quilt covering our canvas window moving and realized a wolf was coming in through the hole! Just as a snarling head pushed the covering aside, a deafening boom coincided with an emptied window; then the yelping pack could be heard retreating up the hill. Etta cautiously opened the door, stepped out and fired again. I hated to think what might have happened if we hadn't had Barrett's gun, or if I had been alone. I was surprised at Etta's cool action in a terrifying situation. She told me that an uncle taught her to shoot; every day I appreciated her more. In the spring I asked Etta to teach me how to shoot, so at least I could protect my little family. Etta skinned the wolf she shot, and sold the pelt. She tried to give me the money but I told her to put it in her money jar.

"Moses came to town twice in March, each time bringing small 'pokes' or bags of gold. After Barrett died, Moses asked me to take care of his share of the gold until summer, and that winter we each already had a sizeable amount in the bank. Mr. Holder, the manager, sent another draft for one hundred dollars to Mother. In some ways her burden had eased with Jim's death in January, and Emily went back to school. I remember thinking that if I got nothing more out of that remote place than a better life for Mother, everything that happened was worth it. I appreciated how Mr. Holder helped with my financial affairs; he was very kind, yet his wife continued to ruthlessly snub me. It was even worse when Etta was with me; Molly saw it happen in her shop one day, and told Mrs. Holder she would have to find someone else for her dressmaking. I was horrified that Molly's stance would hurt her business, and she waved me away, saying 'We have a waiting list of ladies, I am not worried.'

"I usually received a letter or two each time the U.S. post arrived in Dawson. Barrett's father wrote after he received my letter with the sad news of his son's death. I wasn't certain that he believed I was really married to Barrett, but I wrote him back about my pregnancy.

"I spent most of my days with Molly and Esther, sewing dresses and costumes, and trimming fancy hats. A group of society matrons were planning a ball, invitation only of course, for which new dresses were a must. Many of the ladies ordered fancy gowns from Seattle, some even from Paris; however, most needed alterations and they turned to Maison de Mode. It was a good thing the Aunts brought a sewing machine with them, or the work couldn't have been finished so quickly. Etta was indispensible since she took care of pressing the gowns, and delivering them in the buggy. Her pregnancy was difficult to hide, but she had the stamina of her native ancestors and outworked any two of us. Jimmy accompanied Etta on errands after he got home from school; he especially liked taking care of their horse, Brownie. I was so proud of Jimmy and the way he accepted the road bumps in his young life. Molly and Esther absolutely loved him to death, and I think he gained ten pounds in the first month with them. Jimmy never mentioned his mother; I asked if he would like to write her and he just said no, without any explanation. He was quite an intelligent boy, especially in arithmetic, and also excelled in reading.

"The school in Dawson City lacked textbooks for each student, and the one teacher seemed overwhelmed. Sadly, when I approached the school board about teaching some classes, the chairman rebuffed me with a comment about maintaining a strict moral code for the school. I couldn't understand what he had against me. I assumed Barrett was fired as the church pastor for something everyone in town knew about, except me. I thought maybe that my friendship with Kate had been discovered, but I would not give up seeing her.

"Lars was on my mind so much of the time; another miner brought a letter to Jimmy which just said he was fine and asked the Aunts to send a letter back with his friend, with news of everyone. I knew that by the time we saw Lars again, my baby would be born. I felt his movements often, especially at night, and prayed that he would be healthy. Etta told me she was sure my baby was a boy from the way I was carrying it. I had already planned to name him after my father, Nicholas, who I barely remember. Mother had always talked about how kind and smart he was; she became a widow too young, with two small daughters. Now she was widowed for the second time, with three children at home. I thought naming my boy after Father would please her very much. If the baby was a girl, I planned to name her Faith.

"Kate's lover, Alex Pantages, built a new theater, where she starred in her own productions. She laughed at the money she made, saying it was her retirement fund. She was only 24 years old that year, but Kate seemed to know so much about life. The miners loved her; from the gossip we heard, each man swore she was singing right to him.

"Mr. and Mrs. Robertson made Jimmy the best boots he'd ever had, according to him! They stocked a good-sized supply of satin slippers for the ball, which Kate found too tempting!

Tom was kind enough to drop off meat when he went hunting. With so many people in Dawson, there wasn't any game to be found close by. I knew he travelled the frozen river towards Forty-Mile, before he found much to shoot. Some Indians sold dried salmon to whites, and Etta knew how to prepare a sumptuous meal when Tom brought some from the villages. I wasn't sure at the time why he felt obligated to help us, but I certainly appreciated his friendship. The water and firewood deliveries kept Etta and me from having to scramble around to take care of it. We longed to see the spring sunshine again, and I was so anxious to feel the warmth of it on my face. We women were so pale, and since the men shaved their whiskers off during the winters, their faces almost looked grey. I learned that a bearded man would often wake to find his whiskers frozen to his chest! It was very difficult to keep the cabin warm enough to completely disrobe for a full bath, so we made do with basin and washcloth baths. Etta said she also used a banya to cleanse herself, when she visited her sister in the village. It was much like a steam bath: a hut where rocks were heated, on which water was poured. It still sounded too cold for me!

"I found that I need more and more rest. I wished Mother were close by, so I could have asked her about having a baby. Etta planned to go to her sister Asa's cabin about the second week of May, where her baby would be born. While she was gone, I planned to stay with Molly and Esther, since they were worried about my being alone."

"Can you imagine having a baby in a cold cabin?" Rosalie asked Callie.

Callie replied, "Abigail had the option of having a doctor attend the birth of her child, but of course, Etta had to depend on her family."

"Moses was in town for a few days the middle of April, and said water was trickling in little rivulets down the hills. Two weeks later the flumes filled with rushing torrents, and men were ready to sluice the winter dumps and free the gold dust from its winter prison. We needed another man to help Moses, so he hired a middle-aged Irishman, Bricker O'Malley, who'd spent the winter hauling cargo between Lake Bennett and Dawson. Moses was very homesick for his sweetheart in Portland; they wanted to marry and live in eastern Oregon. I was unaware of her existence until he told me a month earlier; Moses said Nora was from the Yakima tribe, and they met while attending the Indian school in Salem. It was hard to imagine running the Black Dog without him, but I agreed we would settle up whenever he wanted.

"With the warmer weather, open ditches along the streets in town were brimming with waste. I'd heard that during the last summer Dawson City also experienced a typhoid epidemic, like there was along the river in the villages. I wasn't surprised, with the filth lying around.

"I had never seen anything as spectacular as the ice going out on the Yukon River the first of May, 1899! There was nothing gradual about it. One day ice covered the river; the next, fearful house-sized slabs were being pushed downstream, with a grinding sound out of hell itself. The force of the river forced slabs up on shore, shattering some river front businesses and cabins. Crowds lined the river front at a safe distance, to watch the sensational show, where whole islands of trees moved among the icy chunks, and portions of the forest were splintered and churned like so many straws. Etta and I stood among the crowd, trying to hide our respective conditions under heavy shawls. Mrs. Holder was just leaving a shop, accompanied by other society matrons, and when she saw us, she turned to whisper to her friends and then pointed. They laughed and flounced past us on the planked sidewalk. Suddenly, Mr. Holder came out of the bank, evidently having seen her actions, marched up to her and gave her (what I would call) an earful. Her jaw dropped open and the ladies with her backed away. I could not hear what he said, but from the gesturing and expressions, it was clear he was angry. I'm sure she will find a way to get back at both her husband, and me.

"A letter from Mother reported good things going on at the ranch. They had ample rain that spring, so the meadows were lush, and cattle were getting fat. Oh, how I would've loved to see Mother's face right then! As if she heard my wish, the next letter contained a portrait of Mother, Emily and the boys.

"One morning about the middle of May, Etta departed for her sister's house, expecting her baby to be born any day, and Lars surprised me with a visit that same afternoon. He helped pack my clothes and soon we descended on the Aunts. Jimmy couldn't get enough of his dad; he went along with Lars to the boot shop and they stopped at the mercantile for a bag of candy on the way back. Lars was in town just until the next day, picking up a supply of meat. Later that night, when everyone was asleep upstairs, Lars and I sat together in a corner of the shop, avoiding sentimental subjects, but wondering what kind of a spring clean up each of our claims would ultimately produce. Moses regularly brought me a little bag of nuggets; while not a fortune so far, we were hopeful. Lars' share of the claim he worked was only twenty percent, out of which he had to pay some expenses. The claim owner had arrived with two more men, so Lars figured he would get paid off in a few weeks. I asked him if he would tell me if he needed money until the clean-up, but he laughed and said "No." Without warning, my baby started kicking hard, and I asked Lars if he wanted to feel it. We sat for a long time, leaning together with his arm around my shoulder and one hand on my stomach. Tears burned my eyes; I wasn't certain whether I was heartsick over our situation, or deliriously happy to have Lars in my life right then. Either way, I tried to keep my emotions in check when Lars said he had never cared for another woman like he did for me. As we started up the stairs he drew me closer than he should have and kissed me soundly on the lips. Oh, that kiss didn't help remove from my head the memory of the night we spent together in Tanana."

Rosalie said, "I am keeping my fingers crossed that it worked out for them to be together. Obviously, they were very much in love."

"I'll take over, Rosalie," offered Callie. "First I need some coffee. What about you two?"

"Definitely need a break, but will skip the coffee!" Rosalie said as she stepped quickly down the hall.

"So, Rosalie told me that you grew up around Antelope," Ray said to Callie.

"Yes, both my husband and I grew up on ranches between Antelope and Ashwood. We married in 1940, lived on his dad's ranch until Pearl Harbor happened. Lem enlisted of course, and I didn't see him for almost four years. He was injured right at the war's end and eventually sent to a hospital in San Diego. We were so excited when Lem finally came home." Callie recalled.

Ray answered, "It is incredible how your families are so linked to this ranching country."

Callie continued, "When we found a small ranch near Prineville, not far from the ranch where Grandma Abigail was raised, she surprised us with the money to buy it. We had our boy and girl there, but when Uncle Bill died, leaving the old Storey ranch to me, it was an answer to my prayers. My parents were still on their ranch near Antelope. Lem and I were so happy living at Shaniko; the years just passed too fast."

Rosalie took her place on the sofa, and asked, "Did I miss anything?"

"I was just getting ready to ask Callie something. So if you inherited the ranch, how are you related to Alice and Russ Storey?" Ray said.

Callie responded, "Can I explain that later? I don't want to introduce you to characters before the fact."

"Sure, I love a mystery!" laughed Ray.

"A letter Abigail wrote to Alice in July of 1899, brought her friend up to date," Callie said, as she opened the next envelope.

July 2, 1899
Dawson City, Yukon Territory

Dear Alice,

I am so sorry it has been so long since I've written. Two little babies keep me very busy! Yes, two babies. I have a darling red-haired daughter who is named Faith, and a husky son, named Nicholas. They were born in my cabin, with some help from Molly and Etta. I feel very fit, but Etta will not let me lift a finger to do any heavy work. Her baby was born the end of May, but died, and we're very sad; however, she is feeling better. I don't know what I would do without her; our very existence here is so intertwined. I purchased a high-backed rocker, and it seems that one of us is always sitting in it with a tiny baby cuddled close.

My gold mine is paying out successfully; so much so that I've invested in a new steam thawing machine. It's so much faster than building small fires directly on the permanently frozen gravel. Of course, this means we need more workers at the site, so I now employ six men. Moses is leaving in a week to begin a new life in Oregon; I offered to have the mine appraised and buy out his share, but he only wanted half of what had been deposited in the bank. He has been a loyal friend and I'll not soon forget him.

Kate is the most popular entertainer in the whole Klondike District. I see her often, usually at Molly and Esther's shop. She is a dear, and dotes on the babies. Between Kate, Etta, Esther, and Molly, my children are treated like a prince and princess!

News has reached Dawson City of a huge gold strike on Anvil Creek in western Alaska Territory, near Cape Nome. A large number of Klondike prospectors have headed downriver, mostly those who do not have their own claims here. Lars Jensen says that he might go, since the claim he worked on this winter is being abandoned and he's been working day labor up on Gold Hill Creek. He has some income from the drawings he makes and sells to miners, saloon girls, Mounties, and matrons. Photographs are very popular, but Lars' drawings make the women prettier, men more handsome and miners less scruffy. He is at loose ends, has little money, and hasn't been to town for several weeks; I suppose it is his pride. If he follows the Nome strike, I hope he lets Jimmy stay with the Aunts for awhile longer. I do love Lars so much, but realize that I may have to make another life for my children, since Lars is out of my reach. We have much that ties us together, but that's not enough for Faith and Nicholas. Sometimes I think I have made a mess of things; one year ago I left Prineville as a naïve girl. I should have turned around in St. Michaels; however, several people rely on me now, so I have to face forward. You've probably realized that I have decided to stay another year; my claim is producing a moderate amount and I will need the money when we do return to Oregon.

I've come to think of Etta like a real sister. She is of a diminutive stature; however she has the strength of a titan. Since her father was white, she has a lighter complexion than most Indians, and more refined features. Occasionally I can get her to plait her long black hair into two braids which are then wrapped across her head, or made into a bun, much like I do when going to town. Most days, she pulls the loose mane back to the nape of her neck, and ties it with a leather thong. She wears the same type skirts and shirtwaists as I do, but chooses to wear only moccasins on her feet. Indians usually make their parkas with the fur on the inside; women, and some men wear a bright fabric tunic over it. She keeps a tidy cabin, so I have no reservations about her caring for the babies. Etta is smart and I offered to help improve her reading and writing, to which she responded, "Maybe."

Your letters are read and re-read! Although Etta doesn't know you, she will repeatedly ask to have the letters read aloud, over and over. The portrait you sent of your little family sits on the shelf next to the one of Barrett and me.

Your friend,
Abigail

I X

· ·

"SO SHE HAD TWINS! DOES THIS WOMAN EVER GET A break?" Ray exclaimed. Callie broke into a hearty laugh, and said, "I told you, she was tough!"

"Would you like for me to read awhile, Callie?" Rosalie offered.

"No, I will for now," Callie said, as she picked up the memoir. Rosalie nearly asked her why she skipped ahead in the journal, beyond the place marked where they left off. Then she thought better of it; after all, Callie had warned them the memoir held secrets.

"Just before Independence Day the hospital doctors posted bulletins around town, warning about the spread of cholera in Dawson. Almost overnight we had dozens of cases, involving all ages. I couldn't understand why more wasn't being done to clean up the unsanitary conditions in town. Chamber pots were still emptied alongside cabins and boarding houses, drawing flies, and dogs. There were no drains to direct the mess away from water pumps or kitchen doors. At least we lived uphill, with our own privy for use in warm weather, and a place to dump the chamber pots during the winter. I didn't dare go into town until the epidemic was squashed. The hospital was filled with cases, and the survival rate was very low. Finally, an order was enforced that required all slops be dumped in a central pit that was maintained by a health worker. All public water sources had to be certified, or shut down. After about a month, the cholera epidemic was over.

"I had the opinion that Pantages was sweet-talking Kate, just to get access to her money for his theater expenses. She was crazy about him though, and had told me that they planned to marry. As Klondike Kate, the entertainer, she managed to amass a small fortune in nuggets, and was known to often help out destitute prospectors. One late evening a porter from the theater came to fetch me, saying Kate had torn open a seam in a costume and wondered if I could come repair it before her next performance that night. I hurried to her dressing room, and repaired the seam just before the crowd began roaring for her to come onstage. Kate hugged me and bustled out of the room, and I heard her hearty laugh before she broke into song. When I left the dressing room, I glanced up to see her from the wings and couldn't take my eyes off her. Her performance was astounding and totally captivating; I understood why her fans felt a personal connection to Klondike Kate. She sashayed across the stage, waggled her finger at dandies and miners alike, dipped her shoulder and lifted her skirts to show off her garters. Some of her songs were bawdy, but many were nostalgic ballads about sweethearts and mothers. Before I realized how late it was, Kate bowed and I clapped as loud as any in the crowd. She did three curtain calls before I convinced myself I had to return home. Following that experience, when I helped design a costume for Kate, I found it easier to visualize her in front of an audience.

"Hundreds were leaving Dawson every day, headed for Nome, the new name for Anvil City. Marginal claims around Dawson were being sold off to conglomerates to pay for passage to the west, and I'd seen for myself some of the small boats used to float downstream when the men (and women) didn't have steamboat fare. We heard reports that several travelers drowned, and scores were stranded along the Yukon River banks when the boats broke apart.

"Lars came back to Dawson the middle of July and told me he was leaving for Nome the next day. I knew that I couldn't stop him; however, I did convince him to accept a loan so he could travel by steamer, faster and safer, and reach the gold laden beaches quickly. Lars wanted Jimmy to stay in Dawson until he got established, perhaps by summer's end. He asked to see the babies before leaving, and we tip-toed into my bedroom. He stood over them for a few minutes; I could only guess what he was thinking. Finally, he kissed their heads, turned and quickly took me in his arms. Etta was in the next room, and Lars whispered closely that he wanted to see me alone that evening. His embrace was so passionate, and I ached to give in to the desire I felt. Lars pleaded, showered my face with kisses, and reminded me of what we shared last summer. He said we deserved whatever happiness we could make for ourselves. I turned over in my mind what he said and tried to make myself agree with him. Faith squirmed and cried out in her sleep; I pulled away from Lars to tuck the blanket around my little girl. I realized then that we had no future together unless he could free himself from Myra; anything else would not be fair to my children. When I told Lars I first had to think of what was best for them, I thought for just a moment anger flashed behind his eyes, but he smiled and assured me that somehow we would be together. I knew Etta heard some of our conversation, because her eyes were wide and questioning after Lars went out the door. I didn't see him again before his boat left for Nome."

"I wonder if Abby felt that Lars was being selfish, by assuming they could go on with an affair," Rosalie said.

Callie responded, "Grandma Abby was the ultimate mother for her babies, from their first breaths. She was no longer a naïve young girl, looking for a man to take care of her. She wanted Lars, but not at Faith and Nicholas's expense; they deserved a proper father."

"After this, was she always an independent woman?" Rosalie asked.

"Abby told me she wanted a man to lean on when she was tired of thinking, but she reserved the right to disagree with him!" Callie laughed. "Rosalie, would you like to read awhile?"

"I made a marvelous discovery near the end of July. Tom came by the cabin and I invited him for lunch. He went on to tell Etta and I that he had just visited a fellow in the new hospital he'd picked up along the trail last month, who had an awful case of scurvy and was destitute. Tom said he only knew the man by the name of Carnahan, and that he had come north from Oregon. I remembered the little boy who suffered from seizures on the stage, and asked Tom if it would be alright if I visited the man, explaining that I might know his family. That very day I walked down to the hospital, and soon stood at the bedside of a very sick man. 'Are you Archie Carnahan?' I asked. He nodded, astounded that I knew. "Do you have a wife and boy in Oregon?" He immediately teared up, and replied that he did, and wanted nothing more than to see them again. I handed him a small bag of nuggets, and simply said, "Your family loves and needs you. Take this to them with tales of your adventures." He shook my hand and asked who I was, but I just said, "Get well quickly, and catch the fastest steam boat you can find!"

"One thing that threw a negative slant on summertime in the Yukon was the mosquitoes! At least during the colder months we were free of the pests; yet we pined away for sunny days and fields of flowers. Etta was vigilant about tying mosquito netting over the twins' bassinets because even inside the cabin, we were bombarded with attacks. I used lavender oil liberally on my uncovered arms and neck, but Etta claimed clove oil was better to repel the insects.

"Sunday at the Aunts was my favorite day of the week; Ida

Robertson regularly joined us for afternoons of tea and French pastries. Faith and Nicholas were passed from lap to shoulder, with lots of cooing and tickling! Sometimes Etta got her fill of sharing the babies, and took them away with an excuse that they needed diapers changed or such.

"On our way home from sewing with the Aunts one afternoon in August, I pointed out to Etta how beautiful the flower draped hills surrounding Dawson appeared. The slopes looked as if an enormous carpet lay over the landscape; splotches of pink, blue, yellow, purple, every possible color, swirled over the low mounds and valleys. The sun's rays through scattered clouds seemed to spotlight different patches before moving on to another place. I wanted to run through the fields and test my sense of smell with the wild perfumery. Two fretful babies kept my feet on the road, headed for home.

"Etta amazed me with the speed she had improved her writing and reading English. Once she became determined, there was nothing to stop her! I unpacked my school books and made a stack of the ones I thought she could use. In two months that stack was whittled down to half, so I wrote Mother asking her to ship the books on my shelf in the bedroom Emily and I had shared.

"The garden Etta planted in June that year was thriving in the long days of sunlight. Luckily, we didn't have to haul water very often for the plants, since showers came regularly. A few days after we had a fearsome thunderstorm, the sun took on a red cast that looked so strange. The rumor was that a large forest fire was burning south of Dawson City, on ridges above the Klondike River; soon the wind changed direction and blew thick smoke into town, which made even a red sun hard to see. After several more days, misty, cool weather moved into the region and dampened the fires at last.

"A situation came up that forced me to plan a trip to the mine, so I made arrangements to borrow a horse from Tom. I had a detailed map of the route, and remembered most of the forks and landmarks from the trip the previous winter. My foreman had been delivering the gold directly to the bank for deposit every two weeks, and I always picked up the receipt from Mr. Holder a day or two later. I had been so busy with the babies, and sewing costumes for several actresses at the Opera House, I had not stopped by the bank for a few weeks. One morning, on my way to the shop, Mr. Holder met me on the street and said he assumed my claim had played out, since we hadn't brought any gold to the bank for awhile. I was shocked, and told him I would immediately investigate. He advised me to not go to the mine alone.

"Just before Tom brought the horse to me, a visitor at the cabin brought information that meant I didn't have to go to the claim that very day. A young man in my employ told me the foreman, Bricker O'Malley, left for town as he usually did twice a month, to take the gold to the bank, but he hadn't returned after a week. They were short on food, so I told him he did the right thing about coming to me, and gave him money to pick up what they needed. That very afternoon I made a report to the Police Commissioner. I had no idea how much gold was missing.

"I was so angry about the gold stolen from the Black Dog. I should have paid more attention to the mine and not trusted a man of whom I knew nothing, to take care of it. Things were handled differently from that point forward."

"So did she lose everything?" Ray asked.

"Grandma Abigail told me she was stunned when the bank manager told her that no deposits had been made for six weeks. She reported the theft to the Commissioner, who launched an investigation, starting with questioning her other employees. They said that O'Malley left as usual every two weeks, as if he was going to deposit the gold. He would come back in two or three days carrying supplies. It was clear that O'Malley had kept the gold, and now had over a week's head start on his way out of the Klondike. A few days later some men up the Yukon River near Lake Bennett said they had seen O'Malley in a canoe with another man. If they escaped to Skagway and got on a ship to Seattle or San Francisco under false names, there would have been no chance they'd be caught. It was a blow to Abigail's newly found self-reliance, and she said so to her friends. Etta was clearly angry and Abigail thought it wouldn't do for her to be the one to deliver punishment if O'Malley was caught!"

Rosalie asked, "Was he ever captured?"

"Just before freeze-up two bodies were found about a mile apart on the river's banks, one being identified as O'Malley. There was no sign of foul play, so the Mounties determined that the canoe had overturned, the men drowned and the gold was at the bottom of the river. Of course, Abigail was relieved to get the news, but the loss of income was a blow. Go ahead, Rosalie, read what she did next."

"On August 8, 1899, Etta and I packed up the twins, a tent, and supplies to stay at the mine, so I could supervise the diggings myself for awhile. I swore that I wouldn't be swindled by a man again. The days were very long, but I was finally satisfied the operation was efficient, with just a small chance of pilfering. I paid six men good wages, with hot meals prepared by a hired cook. The new foreman and I visited upstream with a mine owner who employed a dozen workers. He gave us some tips about a more efficient flume design, and we quickly noticed a difference in collected gold dust. Although it wasn't very lady-like, I usually pulled on a pair of canvas pants under my skirt, and joined the men at the termination of the flumes. The gold collected in riffles while the lighter dirt was washed away. It appeared that the mine was not producing as much as three or four months earlier.

"Etta managed to make a cozy home for us with the tent and our few furnishings; the twins thrived also and loved the attention shown by miners when resting and eating. A travelling photographer came by the Black Dog one day, so I hired him to get images of the men posing by the mine, before he took several images of the children, Etta and me. Every evening the day's gold nuggets and dust were personally bagged and secured by me. After staying at the mine a month, we packed up and moved back to the cabin, a welcome change. My foreman, Mr. Kratz, handled everything after that, with one difference: he had instructions to bring what they collected each week, directly to me.

"Near the end of September, Jimmy received a letter from Lars. He wanted his son to stay in Dawson again that winter, since Nome was a hotbed of lawlessness. Claim jumping made it impossible to leave for any length of time, but he had made a good strike up the beach about ten miles from the tent city. It was wonderful that Lars finally had success. I suspected that Jimmy was relieved he could stay in Dawson since he had several good friends who did everything together, and that was important for a boy. From what Lars said, Nome hadn't yet built schools or churches, but there were dozens of saloons and gambling halls.

"Etta and I spent many sunny days on the surrounding slopes, picking buckets of ripening berries. Each of us carried a precious baby in a sling, Indian style, so our hands were free to work. Mosquitoes were not so fierce, and as long as we stayed clear of swamps, the tiny biting flies could be avoided. We returned each time with hands stained blue or dark red, proud of the bonanza discoveries of blueberries, raspberries, cranberries, and currants. Our shelves groaned with jars of preserves; Etta also taught me how to dry the fruits on cheesecloth stretched on a frame that was suspended above our heads. Earlier in the summer, when I decided we'd stay in Dawson City another year, I sent an order to Seattle for canned meats, vegetables, milk, sugar, flour…items less expensive purchased 'outside' even with the added shipping costs. The Robertsons and Aunts joined me in making up a larger order, which meant we got a much reduced shipping rate.

"By the first week of November, it was quite cold, and snow was piled deep enough that when Mr. Johnson brought our water, he also shoveled a path from our door to the woodpile. I tried to pay him for this, but he waved it aside, saying he hoped someone would do the same for his wife back home. Horse-drawn sleds ran up and down the main roads to beat down the drifts, but dog sleds were the only reliable way to travel on the creeks to the mines. The crowds in Dawson my second winter differed greatly from what I saw a year earlier. Previously, the planked sidewalks were filled with trades people, prospectors, and gamblers to the point that Etta and I were roughly jostled as we made our way to the Maison de Mode. According to a town census at the end of 1899, there were only about 6,000 souls in Dawson proper, with another 3,000 scattered on their claims. Before the Nome discovery, there were about 25,000 people in Dawson City.

"Sergeant Brant, the Mountie who conducted the investigation on the robbery of my mine, asked me to accompany him to the Provincial Ball held the end of November. I hadn't ventured out of my small circle of close friends, and felt a bit nervous about going. Aside from coming into contact with society women during their visits to Maison de Mode, I avoided putting myself in their line of fire! Mrs. Holder wasn't in Dawson that winter, so at least I wasn't a target of her remarks. Sgt. Brant was very nice, and cut a striking figure in his red coat!

"Esther had gradually become softer, and not so judgmental in affairs of the heart. In the past, she criticized women who became 'daffy' (her word) over men. She seemed to brighten up when Tom Doaks entered the room, and I wondered if his frequent visits to the shop were more to see Esther than to run errands for the rest of us!

"In late December, an early morning rap on the door proved to be Kate, in a state of tears. She blurted that Alex Pantages had broken their engagement, and she was inconsolable. When I got her calmed down, she tearfully told me she thought he had found someone else, someone who was accepted in society. Kate realized that although she was famous and beautiful, her profession kept her from being 'respectable.' I personally knew that Kate was a good person, with flaws like everyone else, but she was unfairly being painted with the same brush as women who lived across the river in Klondike City doing business in the brothels. Jimmy came in the door with our mail, and asked if he could see the babies, so Kate and I changed our conversation. Soon all of us were playing with Faith and Nick on a furry pallet. Etta loved Kate, and the feeling was mutual, but she thought Kate should leave Dawson, and start a new life with a better man. I had to agree.

December 30, 1899
Dawson City, Yukon Territory

Dear Alice,
Your last letter was very welcome, especially since it's been so cold and bleak.

I came under pressure to sell the Black Dog Mine to a conglomerate which is buying out most claims along the creek. No doubt, they will dredge the whole area. Tom said I had to look at the savings that would be realized, since I would not have to make payroll all winter, and the offer was fair. The bank has already sent the funds to the Prineville bank, so I will have a stake to start out when I come home. I miss not having the mine to think about.

My sister, Emily, is excited to be in her final year of high school. I have always promised that I would see she gets to attend a university, and I intend to follow through, no matter the cost. Mother's life is much easier, and the ranch is doing so well that she hired a woman to handle much of the housework. Now she has time to visit her own brothers and sisters.

I wonder if you will have a girl this time, to round out your family. William sounds very much like his father; perhaps a girl will look just like you! One of these years, I hope to see them and my own children playing in your yard, while we share a cup of coffee.

A handsome Canadian Royal Mounted Policeman took me to the Provincial Ball recently, which was the first time I had been "out" since Barrett's death. Molly and Esther designed such a beautiful gown, in dark green taffeta befitting my status as a widow and mother. I had not worn a corset since the babies were born, and was surprised my waist was only 2 inches larger than when I left Oregon. Sgt. Brant declared that I was the most alluring woman at the Ball, which I'm afraid made me blush. He seems interested in seeing more of me; all I have to do is encourage him, I think.

Letters seem to get out of Nome and down to Skagway for delivery to Dawson on the U.S. Mail sleds. Lars wrote that his claim is steadily producing, but he is cautious because the town officials are corrupt. Only the Army stationed nearby provides law enforcement, and even that is not sufficient. The judges and lawyers are only concerned about their own fortunes so some prospectors find they are swindled out of their claims by the very institution formed to protect them. Dawson's newspaper publishes stories about the situation in Nome, warning of the dangers. Construction on a school in Nome is actually underway, and Lars says there are more women and children in Nome than when we arrived in Dawson. He and Jimmy are looking forward to being together again, once the steamers start running the river in late June. The Aunts will miss Jimmy more than I can imagine; he has been a delight to see almost every day and has made us all proud with his success at school.

Faith and Nick are almost six months old; I'll never regret having them, but life seems an endless road of washing diapers, feedings, and trying to keep them warm. Without Etta, all this would be impossible.

Can you believe we are ringing in 1900? Please write again,

Your friend,

Abigail

"I didn't know that Nome was such a wild place, compared to Dawson. What was the reason?" Rosalie asked Callie.

Callie answered, "The Mounties had been active in the Yukon for years, knew the rivers and villages, and had been holding down the law in earlier gold mining strikes. They had requirements for what supplies gold seekers must have to enter the Yukon, to keep men from starving or stealing other prospectors' supplies. They kept a close watch on mining activity, and required that each claim be renewed every year to keep up with abandonments. Very few killings took place in Dawson, although Skagway, in U.S. territory, was quite wild. There wasn't much around Nome until the discovery of gold on the beaches, and judges were more interested in making their fortunes than enforcing laws. Even Wyatt Earp was in Nome, but he left with a lot of money too."

"I'd be glad to read for awhile," offered Ray.

"Sgt. Brant came by once or twice a week that winter, always bringing gifts for Faith and Nick. Storms kept us inside the cabin for days on end, preventing Etta and I from getting to see Molly and Esther. One morning, Tom pulled up at our door with his dog sled in a tumble of barking and yipping. He bundled us all under the fur robes and took us to the shop as a surprise for Esther and Molly. It was a wonderful outing especially for Etta and I after being cooped up so long, and the babies didn't seem to mind a bit. Tom was careful, just trotting the dogs at a leisurely pace; I couldn't imagine riding at the break-neck speeds I've seen on the frozen river. The daylight was lengthening a little at a time, which helped whisk away the doldrums. I learned that day that the Robertsons were making plans to move to Nome that summer, since they both wanted to live in a U.S. territory again. There had been no word from Lars for over two months.

"In February, Tom came by the shop during a Sunday gathering of Kate, the Aunts, Etta, Ida Robertson, the babies and me. Jimmy was at a friend's house for the afternoon, which was just as well. Tom marched into the middle of the crowded room upstairs, and asked if he could speak privately to Esther. She turned and just looked at him for a minute, while the rest of us sat, holding our breaths. Finally Esther said, 'I have no secrets from my friends.' 'Very well,' Tom said, and cleared his throat. 'I am asking you to accompany me to Nome in the summer, as my wife of course.' The room was very still and quiet, and we all turned in unison to look at Esther! She announced, 'I'll have to ask Molly.' Molly laughed and said, 'Silly girl! You better say yes!' Esther melted into Tom's arms and said, 'Yes, Tom, I will marry you and go to Nome!.' We all celebrated that evening with a bottle of champagne Tom thought to bring. Esther had changed into a younger version of herself, and I realized she was not as old as I had assumed. Believing that she would remain an old maid, she usually wore matronly dresses and unfashionable hair styles, until the last few weeks. Etta and I had discussed changes in our friend, including a livelier step. Tom couldn't stop smiling; I was so happy for them! Esther confided to me that she was a bit anxious about the move to Nome, leaving Molly behind, since they had been friends and business partners for so many years.

"Sgt. Brant was assigned patrol in several villages during some weeks that winter. He came to visit on the evenings he was not on duty out of town, and I rather looked forward to our talks. He was a good friend and I tried to keep our relationship just that, two people enjoying each other's company. Etta astutely observed that Mike was sweet on me, which confirmed what I had suspected. It was a fact that I should move on with my life for the sake of Faith and Nick; yet love still had only one face, and it belonged to Lars.

About the middle of January a box from Mother arrived in Dawson City, and we swarmed over the dozens of books, cooing like they were babies to admire. Emily donated some of her favorites since she understood the craving for a good book. When Etta saw four volumes of Alcott titles, her face settled into a satisfied expression, and I felt the same way about the Bronte and Hawthorne novels.

"With temperatures that approached fifty below zero, even a dash to the woodpile meant dressing warmly in my parka, mittens, and boots. One late night, when I stepped out the door into the perpetual winter darkness, I was struck by the keen sharpness of the stars. It was almost like they were frozen diamonds, brittle in the blue-black sky. Abruptly, a blue and white curtain rose from the far-off hills, undulating slowly, growing larger, and changing colors, until white and green bands moved from one horizon to another. The spectacle deserved a symphony of horns and strings, but the night was eerily silent. Etta broke my reverie when she stuck her head out the door, calling 'Miss Abby, you okay?' Yes, I was okay.

"By the end of February, ice on the Yukon was so thick, and the temperature was so low, that holes chopped in it for hauling water kept closing. The men who hauled water spent more of their time re-opening holes, and less time delivering. Etta and I hoarded our supply in the barrel, never knowing when we would get more. One afternoon, I was fretting about not being able to wash my hair for two weeks. Etta sat me down at the table, put a towel around my shoulders, and proceeded to rub corn meal into my scalp! By the time she brushed it out, my hair was refreshed and smelled so much better. That girl was a treasure! To keep warm, we hovered around the stove all day and night. We all slept in the main part of the cabin, since I shut off the bedroom to conserve firewood, and heated just the one room. We read aloud to each other to pass the time: two women sitting at the claw-foot table, one bent over a book and the other sewing.

"Sgt. Brant was assigned to visit several villages that month, and I did miss his visits; however I was uncomfortable that he assumed we were a couple. I just wanted to be friends without the romance.

"We didn't dare take the babies outdoors, so one of us stayed in the cabin with them when the other had to run an errand. One bitter day I suggested that Etta see if the mail carrier had come from Skagway, and go on to the Aunts for a visit. I knew that in addition to buying a newspaper which should have news from Nome, the Aunts would most likely gossip about the ladies in their shop. Etta's news from town gave us a lot to talk about when she returned. Mr. Holder was taking a new position with a bank in Nome that summer. His wife, who has been in Seattle all winter, would meet him in Nome, so we wouldn't see her in Dawson again, which was very good news! Kate had been sick with a cough, but I suspected she was just exhausted. She demanded a lot of herself, saying the audience would be disappointed if she didn't perform. Molly told Etta that the Mounties investigated Kate over an accusation from a miner that she cheated him in some kind of scheme. Nothing could be proven, but I was worried that she was being talked into using underhanded methods to keep accumulating the wealth that she wanted so much.

X

. . . .

April 1, 1900
Dawson City, Yukon Territory

Dear Alice,

We have survived another winter in the Klondike! It was a difficult one, but everybody is healthy and happy. My two cherubs are little darlings. Faith loves to be sung to, and tries to imitate me; Nicholas is learning to climb on everything, which has led to bumps and bruises. Etta is totally devoted to these children, and in her opinion they can do no wrong.

People are still coming in to Dawson, following stories of business opportunities catering to the opulent lifestyle of our numerous socialites. Two couples who came in over the ice from Skagway this winter have added to our little social circle. Bettina Zielinski's husband, Jozef, is a silversmith, and Wolanya Gorski helps her husband, Cyryl, in their art studio. The women have been friends since childhood (like you and I), and right away said they like to be called Tina and Anya. I like them!

Sgt. Brant was away for over a month, and when he returned, his attentions did too. I don't encourage him at all, and I find excuses to avoid being alone with him. The manner of his look is plain; I only wish I felt the same.

I did the most foolish thing, which could have had terrible

consequences! One evening I decided to wash my hair after waiting so long through the coldest of days. The room was frigid, even with a bright fire in the stove; I leaned over the stove to make my long hair dry faster. Suddenly a terrible scorchy smell alerted me that my hair was frying! By the time I realized what was happening, Etta had grabbed a towel and started rubbing the ends to stop the damage. Etta said she would simply trim off the charred parts and she kept cutting and cutting. All I can say is I no longer have waist length hair; it's still long enough to pull it back in a bun, but braids are out of the question. Etta says I'm lucky to have any hair left at all. If it weren't so scary, it would be funny.

Alice, I forgot to tell you about great improvements in Dawson. The town now has electricity (not to my cabin yet), telephones (also not up here yet), sewer and water lines just on Front Street. A telegraph line connects Dawson with Skagway now. What a difference from two years ago! You should see the new homes being built, just like the ones along First Street in Prineville. A railroad will soon be running between Skagway and Whitehorse.

I also hadn't told you that Barrett's parents never contacted me after I wrote them about the twins. I am mystified, but it is their loss. Faith looks so much like her father.

Shaniko must be beautiful, up on the hill with all new buildings. When I rode the stage to The Dalles, I remember we stopped in Cross Hollows for a fresh team, and was told the whole town was moving and being renamed. Is there a school built yet?

My plans for the rest of this year are not clear right now. Sometimes I am very confused about where I want to be.

Your friend,

Abigail

"Esther and Tom were married on May 10, 1900, and she was a beautiful bride! Her dress and hat were made of ecru satin, and she wore kid leather slippers specially made by Mr. Robertson. Tom was so nervous, I was afraid he was going to faint before the vows were finished! They planned to be on the first sternwheeler down the river to St. Michaels, where a ship would carry them to Nome. From what we had learned, Nome was still mostly a tent city, but the construction season had just begun. Both Esther and Tom wanted Molly to join them, but she decided to wait until they assessed the potential for a dress shop there. At that time she had dozens of orders for costumes and ball dresses right in Dawson City. Etta and I were able to make a good living doing handwork for Molly, some that could be done at home in the evenings. As long as I had a monthly income, I didn't have to dig into my savings.

"I wrote Lars that Jimmy would be aboard the same steamer as Tom and Esther. Throngs of people were getting ready to leave Dawson that summer bound for Nome, including the Robertsons. They planned to catch a boat in late July, which gave them time to pack up the whole shop.

"With the warming weather, Etta and I brought all the game meat in our cache into the cabin to slice and prepare for making jerky. Tom built a small smokehouse, and within a week we had cloth bags of meat hanging from the rafters. I became fond of sourdough biscuits and jerky for a quick lunch, and the twins gummed strips of the meat too.

"A letter arrived about this time from my friend Moses, which was a wonderful surprise. He and his wife, Nora, had settled in Pendleton, Oregon, where his share of the Black Dog Mine's gold bought them a home. I wrote him back that we were still in Dawson City, but I had sold the mine. In 1925, I had a chance to see him again, and his easy manner was still the same.

"Kate had been through a rough winter; making money came easy for her, but she was unhappy in love. She and Alex Pantages renewed their engagement for a few months, just long enough for her to invest in a business he started. Alex jilted her soon afterwards. I wasn't in a position to advise her about love; I couldn't even straighten out my own feelings. Mike was pressuring me to return his affection, but I still waited to hear from Lars, dreaming that somehow he would be freed from Myra.

"Etta decided the twins and I should accompany her to her sister Asa's, cabin. We borrowed the Maison de Mode's horse and buggy, since Asa lived about four miles up the Yukon Flats. She was married to a white man, so they could live anywhere they chose. The two sisters were very much alike, so I enjoyed the visit immensely. Etta insisted that I join her in the large banya, for a steamy cleansing. The whole process was wonderfully relaxing, and I never felt so refreshed!

"Alice's letter announcing the birth of their new son took just three weeks to reach Dawson, which was a record at that time. They named him Cal, after his grandfather Storey.

"Dawson's streets were deep in mud in May, with no chance of drying up with the rain we'd been having for weeks. Skirt hems became brown mops, obscenely wiping plank sidewalks in wide swaths. When dry, skirts were beat against a door or table leg, which covered the floor with chips and clods, which in turn were swept out the door to melt into mud again. After a long, dark winter, I craved summer days when merely a shaft of sunlight through the doorway lifted my spirits and burned away the cobwebs in my head. Etta and I loved to sit on our outside bench, with Faith and Nicholas at our feet, letting the solar elixir work its way into the marrow of our bones. One would think that since we had to endure the bitter winters, the short summers should guarantee day after day of brilliant warmth. Imagine my dismay on June 1st when I woke to find a cloak of fog and light rain wrapped over the hills. I knew the sun lurked on the far side of those clouds, wasting it's warmth on neither an animal nor plant. Etta suggested we make taffy, and take some to the Aunts; she always knew my moods and what perked up my day. The babies played with small strings of the candy, and of course some went on the floor, but it entertained us all. After the twin's naps, we gathered up to take the wrapped candy to town; the mist had disappeared except for some pushed around on an occasional puff of wind. By eight o'clock that night, the Klondike sun was out in all its glory, so we sat on our bench after the twins were asleep. Sometimes, I felt sorry for myself, but not that day.

"All of our friends came to the cabin for Faith and Nick's birthday party in June, perhaps a bit silly since they were so young, but I think all of us needed a good time before Esther, Tom and Jimmy left. Sgt. Brant paid a lot of attention to the twins, and they begged to sit on his lap.

"One of the young miners who worked for me last fall asked if I had anything he could do to make a little money. Frank Collins was working at odd jobs around town, saving up for boat fare to Nome. The cabin roof needed repairs before winter, so I hired him for that job, and also paid him to cut and stack several cords of wood. Mr. Johnson and his brother, who always took care of our water and firewood, left for Nome, so I bought his wagon since Frank said he could borrow a horse from his cousin when we needed to haul wood or water.

"Anyone observing my preparations for the next winter would have assumed I was staying in Dawson. There was still a chance I would go on to Nome before winter, but I had to be ready either way.

"Kate decided to travel 'outside' for a few months with Pantages. I had mixed feelings about losing so many old friends to Nome or further south. The excitement each one showed when describing plans and dreams forced me to be happy for them. I envied each one, because they had chosen to expose their lives to new and daring events. My life seemed to exist in a bubble, while I tip-toed around commitments and pined for things I thought I wanted, but were out of reach. If Mother had been there, I am sure she would have said to quit being 'wishy-washy'!

"By the middle of August, Dawson had been gripped in a typhoid epidemic for two months. Etta and I kept Faith and Nick away from town; one of us at a time walked to Molly's for an afternoon of sewing, and we brought home pieces of handwork. Our only outings with the children were toting them into the purple hills above the cabin, walking among the lupines and columbines. Rolling around in the meadows filled with buttercups and kinnickkinnick would pitch Faith and Nick into fits of giggling. One day a memory pushed its way up from the back of my mind: I was playing in a beautiful meadow, being watched by a shadowy man, who must have been my father. I was happy, so happy.

"During the epidemic Frank, our handyman, brought water from a creek far up the hill from our cabin, where no one lived above. Etta and I did everything we could to protect the children. Some restaurants closed down, which probably helped from spreading the disease further; we let Frank stay at the cabin with us, to avoid being exposed to the germs. The two hospitals were overwhelmed with desperately sick people, and they reported that fifty-two people died; many more had lasting ailments from the assault on their bodies. I hoped that some of the city officials would do something about the unsanitary conditions still plaguing the town.

"So many girls who worked the saloons and theaters were struck down in the epidemic; it was indeed a blessing that Kate chose that particular time to be away from the Klondike. A report was circulated that the brothels across the river suffered horrible losses; a sad ending for those lost women. I wasn't certain that their deaths were even included in Dawson's fatality count.

"With so much time on our hands, Etta and I expanded the garden plot, and ate radishes and lettuce for weeks. By the end of August we dug potatoes, beets, carrots and onions. There was more than enough for us and our close friends."

August 25, 1900
Dawson City, Yukon Territory

Dear Alice,

Once again, it's been too long since I've written. Dawson was gripped with an epidemic, and I was so worried that I couldn't think about writing you a happy, newsy letter. Does little Cal take after you or Russ? I am sure William is going to be a helpful big brother, but there's sure to be jealously at times. Don't worry too much about it, they will work it out.

You must be very proud of Russ with the progress he's making with new strains of sheep being introduced to the herd. I suppose I'm just a ranching girl at heart, since your descriptions of the improvements and even what your days are like, make me homesick.

I know you expected me to return to Oregon by the fall; however, the children and I will remain here in the Klondike this winter. Molly needs an assistant in the shop, since her reputation has resulted in more business than she can handle alone. Etta is an essential link in the business, helping me with the children, and contributing beautiful needlework. Another reason for my reluctance to leave the north is that I have decisions to make concerning Lars and Sergeant Brant. I cannot leave and hope to resolve what hangs on my heart, from 3000 miles away.

Mother is the happiest I have ever known her to be. Emily moved to Forest Grove, to attend Pacific University, which makes me so proud. My little brothers are good boys, according to Mother, and have become more helpful on the ranch.

A note arrived from Nome yesterday, in which Lars advised me that Jimmy arrived safe and sound. Lars' message contained nothing personal about us; I suppose he is very busy, getting Jimmy settled and ready for school. I don't even know if he has a house in town, or has hired men to work his claim.

Kate's absence from Dawson City is noticed by her fans, and some placed advertisements in west coast newspapers, asking her to return soon. She wrote from San Francisco, excited about Pantages' plans to build a chain of theaters in several California cities. I am afraid that his big plans are being financed by her Dawson earnings. It's really none of my business, and I shouldn't gossip, but it's hard to just stand by and listen. I would have more faith in the proposition if he would marry Kate.

If it weren't for new friends Tina and Anya, our Sunday afternoons at Molly's would be quiet indeed. They love to hear our stories of what Dawson was like at the beginning of the rush.

Hug William and Cal for me!

Your best friend,

Abigail

"Well," Callie said, "this is a good stopping place. How about having a bite of lunch?"

"I thought I'd take you gals out to your favorite local restaurant," Ray said.

"My favorite place to eat is at my friend's house! Caroline is going to show up any minute with her famous smoked sausage casserole, and I've already got a layered salad in the fridge", Callie informed them. "It was always Lem's favorite."

Rosalie said, "It sounds good to me! Can I help with anything?"

Caroline arrived and the four of them had a lively lunch, talking about Grandma Abigail. Caroline remembered her, since she and

Callie had been best friends since high school. Caroline said, "Her stories about the Klondike and other places in the north were the most adventurous tales I had ever heard from a real person. And she knew how to tell a good story!"

Callie agreed, "I never got tired of listening."

Caroline asked, "Remember when she would talk about watching men and women traveling up and down the frozen Yukon River?"

"Oh, yes," Callie said, turning to Rosalie and Ray, "Abigail told us that even during the coldest months, dozens of travelers each day could be seen using dogs with sleds, horses pulling sleighs, and even bicycles! Several women ran their own businesses, hauling supplies to miners by dog sleds, up the Yukon and its tributaries."

"I can't believe that people could stay outdoors for very long in the cold temperatures," Ray said. "Maybe they just got used to it."

"From what Abigail said, when it warmed up to twenty below zero, folks poured out of their cabins and tents in just their shirt-sleeves, like it was balmy!" Caroline laughed.

After cookies and coffee, Caroline packed her dishes, and told Callie she'd see her in a couple of days. Rosalie had the casserole recipe in her purse, anxious to make it for Penny's family.

Callie asked, "Rosalie, would you like to read from the memoir for awhile?"

"I'd be glad to!" she replied.

"In October something happened with Michael Brant which hurt and shocked me. And worst of all, I wondered if it was partly my fault. I never meant to lead him on, or play the tease, but he accused me of just that. One Friday night he took me to the Firemen's Ball, for which I wore a new dress and had Etta use the curling iron to style my hair. I had so enjoyed getting out and meeting new people. Michael complimented me, and seemed proud to have me on his arm. When he took me home, Etta was asleep with the children in the bedroom. Mike closed the door so they wouldn't awake while I reheated coffee for the two of us. He led me to the cot where Etta usually slept, gesturing to sit beside him. A moment later his arm was around my shoulder as he drew me close for a kiss. I jumped to my feet, and said, 'Mike, I'm not ready for any more than what we have right now.' He wrenched me down, pushed me back on the cot, as I struggled to get away. He managed to kiss my neck; then I felt his hand under my skirt, pushing aside the layers of petticoats. As I fought him, he sneered, 'It's not like you haven't done this before.' Suddenly, from behind Mike, I heard a metallic click; he pushed away from me and turned his head to see Etta standing outside the bedroom door, with Barrett's shotgun aimed at him. 'You leave now, Sgt. Mike!' Etta angrily said. He threatened, 'I'll have you arrested for this!' I was afraid for her, knowing he could easily make trouble for an Indian. But she just smiled, and replied, 'If you do, my brothers will make sure you never have babies. I think its better you leave Dawson.' As he went out the door, he turned and said to me 'It's your fault, you know!' Etta hugged me as I cried myself to sleep. For two days I avoided leaving the cabin; finally I went to the shop, and learned that Sgt. Brant had transferred to Lake Bennett for the rest of the winter. When Molly told me, she looked to see what my reaction would be; I just shrugged."

Rosalie shuddered, and didn't have anything to say for a few minutes; Ray shifted in his chair, unsure of what to say. Only Callie found a voice in the matter. "Grandma Abigail heard later that Sgt. Brant soon took a post in Alberta. Evidently he wanted to distance himself from Etta's brothers. What's funny is that she didn't have any brothers!" That broke the ice, so Rosalie and Ray could laugh and relax. Callie said that Abigail was more cautious after that attack, and held back from being overly friendly with men, even Tina and Anya's husbands.

X I

. . . .

"I WROTE TO LARS AGAIN, BUT RECEIVED NO REPLY. I was worried that he was sick or injured. Nome had terrible storms hit one right after the other; many beach claims were washed away, right along with the gold-bearing sand. The Klondike Nugget reported that dozens of crimes were committed each week in Nome; surely Lars hadn't been a victim in a shooting. Esther and Tom finally wrote that they had seen Lars just one time since their arrival, but they had Jimmy move from the rooming house to their extra bedroom.

"When snow started falling that year, it came with a vengeance. One morning in November we woke to a fourth day of constant snowfall that dimmed the pink sunrise. It was accumulating inch by inch, so by evening we had three feet on the level. Frank kept our path stomped down with the horse he borrowed, and made sure we had a stack of dry wood inside the cabin at all times. Before the cold weather set in he installed real glass windows to replace the greased canvas. I loved peering out to see who was coming up the trail, or just watching the snow fall. Some evenings I could even watch the northern lights from the comfort of my cabin. One day right after the snow storm Anya's face appeared in my new window, after I was startled by her loud knock. She heard we wouldn't be working in the Maison de Mode for a few days; instead, Etta and I were busy embroidering undergarments for a young lady's trousseau. I hadn't seen Anya for some time, so we had a lot of catching up to do. She had been nursing a bad cough, but some medicine the doctor gave her seemed to help.

"Frank and Etta spent hours talking about his home in Colorado. He was born in Cripple Creek during the gold rush in the '70's. His family found enough gold to pay for a farm near Fort Collins, in the foothills of the Rocky Mountains. Frank didn't want to be a farmer, so when his cousin, Samuel Collins, asked if he wanted to go to the Klondike, he didn't hesitate. In Dawson, Samuel taught at the school, but spent the vacation months working at a mine. The cousins shared a room in a boarding house; I decided to have them for dinner soon.

"Molly came for a visit one evening, since she missed seeing the children during our extremely cold weather. She sat both of them on her lap, and rocked until their eyelids drooped. When she slipped out the door with her lantern, I accompanied my friend part of the way down our hill. On the way back, I couldn't help noticing the pure mass of stars blanketing the sky. With no moon tonight, I could see more than the usual pin points of light. Beyond those stars, I could see patches of silvery gauze, very faint, but there nonetheless. If those patches were made up of more stars, there must be millions. It was very hard to think about such a number, because it made me wonder if each of those stars, like our own sun, had another earth. Perhaps I was thinking too hard, and should've just appreciated the beauty of the night. To this day, I regard the heavens as an infinite source of wonderment.

Rosalie interrupted, anxious to share an observation, "I think Abby had a sense of curiosity about the world around her that was unusual for women at that time. Am I right?"

"Yes, you are right. And she encouraged her children, nieces and nephews to explore and question everything," Callie said, as she took the memoir to read.

"The twins tore into the Christmas presents we had wrapped so carefully! Molly, Etta and I sat back, sipping mulled cider, and watching Nick run his toy wooden horse along the rugs. Faith's favorite was the ballerina music box that Molly gave her; we took turns winding and winding it for her! I wished I could recall more about my sister and brothers when they were small, to compare my own children's habits and skills. I'd seen Nick help his sister figure out problems, like untying the string which kept a cabinet door closed, and Faith could charm him into sitting still while she brushed his hair. Etta and I could watch them play all day long.

"In January Molly received a letter from Nome, with news that Esther and Tom were going to have a baby in May! Molly cried when she told me, and I was so sad when she told me about the baby she had twenty years earlier. I knew she was a widow, but she had never spoken of having a child. She lost both her son and husband in a measles epidemic, and I didn't know what to say. As usual, Molly pulled herself up straight, dabbed her eyes, and said 'Life goes forward, not backwards.'

"When I closed my eyes at night, when the day's noise and activities were put to rest, my mind drifted to Lars and Jimmy. Just a short note, wishing us a Merry Christmas, had arrived at Molly's so I knew they were well. I thought perhaps Lars decided he must honor his marriage, albeit long distance. Since we had no proper future together, I decided he probably wanted to spare me from a dead-end affection; at least, that's what I told myself. In the daylight, if I thought about it, my affair with Lars wasn't so pretty.

"Kate wrote that she and Alex would return in March of that year. From Skagway, the railroad could take them to Whitehorse, and from there they'd hire a sled to run the final 400 miles to Dawson. Etta and I were so happy Kate was coming back; we missed her lively stories, and infectious laugh.

"Frank and Samuel Collins came to dinner twice during the holiday season, which I agreed to do just for Etta. She loved to show off her skill in the kitchen, and I have to say, the things she could do with a plain piece of moose, or fowl, surpassed any chef. I had seen Etta's large black eyes watching Frank as he hauled wood from the wagon, cleaned the stove pipe, or simply played with the twins. In turn, Frank's eyes followed Etta when she stirred a cake batter, or rocked Faith to sleep in the afternoon. Sometimes, days would pass when he was elsewhere, hired out for work. Since we were honest with each other, I asked Etta if she was afraid she'd be compromised again. 'No, Abby, I am not a silly girl anymore. I am like you, careful with men!' And that was that!

"Samuel Collins was a very quiet, but interesting man. He talked very little about himself but made everyone else feel comfortable talking about their own interests. Sam and Frank had been in the Klondike District only since December, '99, so they questioned Etta and me about Dawson City before their arrival. Frank had already told Etta that Sam's wife and baby died in Colorado three years earlier, during childbirth. He was very attentive to the twins; I thought it would make him sad, seeing them so healthy and happy, but he genuinely liked to play with them.

"It was wonderful to have daylight at my disposal again in March! The land was still locked in winter, crispy and white, and the sun glanced off brilliantly clean snow on our hill, which was not yet sullied by spring thaw. Along Dawson City's streets, the only time the snow was clean was right after a new snowfall. The children were so restless one day, we bundled them up on the small sled and headed for town. We veered off to the river where several Indian women were cleaning whitefish caught through the ice. They tossed entrails far out on the ice, where meat-eating birds fought for the tidbits. Large ravens bullied smaller hawks out of the way, and then scuffled with each other, pulling apart the entrails. Lurking on a spruce tree limb, waiting for the perfect moment, a bald eagle sat as still as a stump. Suddenly, he launched off the limb, casting his huge shadow over the scene; as graceful as a well-handled kite, he glided over the ice and landed near the ravens and smaller birds. The ravens' haughty demeanor abruptly changed as the eagle strutted closer, and accessed the meal simply by following the suddenly vacated avenue. He seemed in no hurry, but kept an eye on the greedy birds. If one bravely tip-toed up behind him to pick up a stray morsel, he only had to spread his wings a little to send a warning. Finally satisfied, the magnificent bird of prey strutted and flapped his way farther out on the frozen river, and watched from a distance as the ice was stripped clean. My children, like their mother, were mesmerized.

March 12, 1901
Dawson City, Yukon Territory

Dear Alice,

Why am I so stupid? Can't I see anything coming? I am as blind as the village girls who trust the white men, and the saloon girls who think everyone loves them because they have a "heart of gold."

I stopped by Anya's art shop to have my new photograph of the twins framed. I looked through some samples of frames, and then noticed a black and white sketch leaning against the wall. It depicted miners on the Nome beach, and I recognized the artist as Lars. I asked Anya who brought it in, and she said a man who just arrived from Nome boasted that a friend drew it for him, just before the artist left Nome to get married in California. I said she must have heard wrong, since I knew he was already married. I hurried to Molly's shop, and scared her with the look on my face. She thought something had happened to the twins, and began wringing her hands. I realized what Anya told me actually wasn't the worst thing that could happen, and assured Molly the babies were alright.

After Molly heard about the man in Anya's shop, she ran next door to see if a copy of the latest Nome Nugget newspaper was available. I couldn't bring myself to look, so Molly pored over the pages; sure enough, Lars was married last month in Sacramento. "Isabel Ann Morgan, of Sacramento, California, daughter of Judge Leo Morgan, was united in marriage to Lars Jensen of Nome, formerly of Dawson, YT. Mr. Jensen operates two mining concerns in Nome. After a honeymoon in New York City, the couple will reside in their new home in Sacramento, but they plan to visit Nome frequently while overseeing his business."

How can I ever understand this? Was it true that he was even married? And why did he let me think he loved me? Etta, knowing all my secrets, shares my bewilderment. I never dreamed I would be so betrayed. At first I cried; then I became numb and didn't care. Now, I doubt every decision I've ever made: coming to Dawson, falling in love with Lars, marrying Barrett, trusting Michael Brant, staying in Dawson. What was I thinking, staying here after Barrett died?

I can't bear to leave the cabin. You must forgive me for writing such a letter; I probably should not even mail it; but it helps to talk this out with someone far away. Mother doesn't need to hear this part of my so-called life. Molly knows that I had feelings for Lars; Etta knows that I loved him. But now I never want to see him again. Next time I write, I promise to have better news of my situation.

Your best friend,
Abigail

P.S Please don't worry about me.

"How could he do that to her," Rosalie said, through thin lips. "He didn't even have the guts to write her about an engagement."

"Grandma Abigail told me that she did get a letter from Lars, a few weeks later," Callie told them.

"What was his excuse for being such a jerk?" Ray asked.

Callie laughed at Ray, and sat up straighter in her chair, "We will never know…Grandma burned it without opening! She said there was nothing he could say to make her feel better, and he might have said something that would hurt her more."

"Did Abigail ever see Lars again?" asked Rosalie.

"Patience, Rosalie, patience." Callie answered.

"My job with Molly was a life-saver, giving me a place to go and something to think about besides myself. The twins also made me so happy; their darling faces begged to be kissed, with trust and innocence that glowed in their eyes. They both were so cute…at least Etta and I thought so. Faith had the same red curls as her father, but her eyes were brown, with long lashes. Nicholas took after my side of the family, with light brown hair; he had a slender build whereas Faith was still a chubby toddler. Two years earlier I was unsure about becoming a mother; yet after their births, the children filled my waking hours with wonderment, and my dreams with hope.

"Spring was in the air by April, although winter still held a grip on the hills. Nothing happened gradually in the north; winter hit with a vengeance in a matter of days and summer debuted with the crashing of river ice. When I think of it, my life was much like that: for long periods, stillness enveloped my mind, like winter, followed by bursts of thrilling happiness or utter despair.

"Kate's arrival in Dawson was bittersweet: she came alone, and was much stressed that Alex Pantages stayed behind to work on his theater plans. She confided that her income from performing in Dawson City was essential to finance their projects. When I told Kate about Lars, her jaw actually dropped open in shock, and she could only say, 'No!' But she listened to the details, so finally she knew as much as I did. When I assured her I had closed that chapter of my life, she raised an eyebrow, but quickly veered off to talk about costumes for her new acts. Later, Etta observed, 'Miss Kate's visits makes our days happier. Too bad she is only pretending happiness for herself.' As usual, Etta was right: Kate bubbled into a room, and soon had everyone feeling better. She tried to dismiss the lack of communication from Alex as his being so busy. I'll admit I was a cynic regarding men then, but I knew of no reason to trust Pantages.

"Anya and her husband told all of us that they must leave Dawson as soon as they could pack and arrange passage. She had a lung ailment which was affected by the cold so they decided to relocate to the year- long warmth of Arizona Territory. Tina's jewelry business was thriving; her husband was wonderfully skilled at designing unusual pieces using combinations of gold and silver. Tina encouraged him to import small watches to make into lapel pieces for women, which became very popular around town.

"Maison de Mode became the place to meet for society matrons. Molly acquired patterns and fabrics from New York that rivaled anything Paris had, and we worked feverishly on orders. Cream silk was all the rage for expensive undergarments, but it required a delicate touch. Molly stocked an ample supply of these fragile items, but there were always requests for custom made garments. Etta mastered the sewing machine, something that scared her at first. She grew into a sewing madwoman, able to make a skirt in one afternoon, so Molly bought another machine.

"Dawson saw an influx of prospectors with the spring weather, although they were soon disappointed to find that placer gold was a thing of the past. Even Nome was finished for the small operator, unless men wanted to search the hills for pockets of gold, which was like finding a needle in a haystack. Samuel Collins had a friend who was doing just that, but with just moderate success. He wanted Sam and Frank to join him out in western Alaska Territory and Frank said they had almost made their grubstake. Etta didn't like to talk about Frank leaving for Nome; I hoped she wasn't setting herself up for a big disappointment.

"On May 3rd, Samuel invited all of us to attend the high school graduation ceremony on Sunday. Etta and I wore our nicest dresses and bonnets; she even wore low-heeled ladies' slippers instead of moccasins, after a week of practicing how to walk gracefully. Etta was quite a beautiful woman with clear olive skin, dark eyes, and her white father's demeanor (that is to say Etta did not consider herself less worthy than anyone else). Frank couldn't take his eyes off her. Inside the school, I was suddenly reminded of the time I spent teaching ranchers' children. I missed it more than I realized. Sam presented a diploma to each of the twenty graduates, and after a choral program, he joined our little group. He praised Etta for her determination to continue learning, and she absolutely glowed. Sam was a very kind man, and always knew what a person needed to hear.

"The ice pack on the Yukon River formed a massive jam, and caused flooding in the main part of Dawson on May 15th. It was with hopeless hearts that we watched the water crawl up the banks, higher and higher, onto the streets, into some businesses. All the townspeople worked to protect the buildings; some were saved, and some were moved off their foundations, or collapsed into their own basements. Molly's building was saved. The Orpheum Theater sustained some damage, but Kate said it was nothing that would stop their performances. Thank goodness the water didn't reach First Street where Tina and Anya's shops were. The ice jam had to be dynamited to keep the whole town from being swept away, and afterwards the ice rumbled and grumbled as gigantic chunks tumbled past town.

"Anya and Cyryl had everything packed to be shipped south as soon as the steamers could get down the river. A bon voyage party for the Gorski's was planned, but we all were worried about the way Anya looked; she had dark circles around her eyes, and was very thin.

"Frank and Sam were up the Bonanza, hired for day labor at a large mine. We missed having them in town, but with the new stage service between the creeks and Dawson City, they promised to get back often.

"The June day we celebrated Faith and Nick's birthdays was perfectly warm, with blue skies filled with horse tail clouds. Two ladies I met at the shop brought their children to the party, which made for a busy afternoon! It was always amazing to me that Faith and Nick were so adept at sharing and playing well with other children, when most of their time was spent with adults who indulged their every desire. Their vocabularies were growing along with their bodies, and we had to be careful what was said since it might get repeated to the wrong person.

July 3, 1901
Dawson City, Yukon Territory

Dear Alice,

The Klondike District has changed greatly since I first arrived nearly three years ago. With the arrival of steam boats up the Yukon, disgorging hundreds of men and women, I have noticed a marked difference between these travelers and those of prior summers. Gone are the rough, unshaven prospectors, bent under packs containing their worldly possessions, with pickax handles sticking out at the top, jumping off boats into ankle-deep muck. Instead, we encounter suited businessmen with their ladies, bright-eyed laborers and shopkeepers, and government men carrying brass-trimmed leather cases exiting their boats onto plank docks that are erected each summer after the ice goes out. When Etta and I walk the twins to Maison de Mode, we are no longer approached by hungry prospectors asking for money to buy a meal.

Restaurants rival any in San Francisco, and prices have come down, due to an easing of transportation problems. Galas held in new mansions attract members of high society, who in turn need beautiful dresses and hats. Dawson City's population may have diminished, but the flow of money has not. Kate told me that lavish men's parties are held in dance halls' private rooms, without a thought about the expense. There is no end to the obscene waste of money.

Mother writes that the ranch lost a few cattle during a blizzard this winter, but calving went well. She surprised me with the news that Mr. Carter, a local cabinetmaker who lost his wife a few years ago, has been seeing her home from church, staying for dinner. I am glad she has someone. Emily is home over the summer, helping on the ranch; however, she will return to Pacific University in the fall. Emily included a note that she appreciates so much that I've made it possible for her to attend college. My sweet sister excels in her classes, of which I am very proud. I am quite surprised at her choice of career: she wants to travel the world as an archaeologist! If that's what she wants, then that's what she will get!

Esther and Tom Doaks, who moved to Nome last year, had a baby boy in May. Esther is still in the state of thinking she is the only woman who has had such a beautiful baby. Truthfully, we all are thrilled that she is so content. Tom's teamster business is growing steadily, and they have built a new home. Esther was so sure that she would never marry and have a family; I guess none of us can be certain of anything. They have convinced Molly that Nome is primed for a new dress shop.

On a sad note, my friend Anya Gorski died in the hospital here. She never had the chance to move to Arizona Territory. Cyryl says Anya had a cancer. Tina was able to tell Anya before she died, about the baby they are expecting.

Frank and Sam Collins come to the cabin often, on their trips to town. Frank and Etta are definitely "stepping out," and I couldn't be happier. Sam has asked me out to nice restaurants twice. Most fellow diners, being new to Dawson, know me just as the widow who sews at Maison de Mode. No whispering behind hands or snickering when I pass on the street now. Sam tested how I felt about Frank and Etta marrying and a possible move to Nome. The thought of Etta leaving stunned me. I suppose I must accept that she will want to follow her husband wherever he goes.

Mother wants me to return home soon; however, I need to wait until I see what Etta and Molly will do. I think the North has cast a spell on this old girl.

Your best friend,

Abigail

P.S. I have to say I rather enjoy Sam's company.

"I wonder if she and Sam strike up a romance," said Rosalie.

Callie responded, "She was wary of that. Being burned again wasn't something she would risk."

X I I

· ·

"MY DEAR FRIEND ETTA SAT BESIDE ME ON OUR bench overlooking the river one night right after Independence Day, after the twins were put to bed. I could tell she ached to tell me something, since she kept readjusting her skirt, and looking at her hands. Helping her out, I said, 'So, I think Frank plans to take you with him to Nome.' I patted her hands, and looked right at her; she had tears on her cheeks as she said, 'I love him, Abby, and he wants us to marry.' I told her I knew that, and of course she should marry and go with him. She said, 'But, I can't leave you and the babies. I want Frank to stay here, so we are all together.' We talked long into the evening, about love and commitment, family and friends. I had the same problem thinking of when I would eventually leave Dawson City, and my good friends. Etta had a big decision to make and I couldn't do it for her. I slept little until the early morning hours; finally, in a drowsy dream world, I knew what to do.

"I decided that Molly's plan to move to Nome would also include my little family, and Etta and Frank as a married couple! Etta was so committed to Faith and Nick, she would have never left without them, so I was forced (happily) to get off the fence and make up my mind! Frank considered staying in Dawson since he understood Etta's feelings; she told him everything that happened over the last three years. I couldn't let him miss this opportunity, nor did I want Etta sad if he left. Molly was ecstatic that I would help move her shop to Nome, and continue to be part of that business. I thought a lot about the decision, but Nick and Faith would never have understood if Etta was not part of their everyday lives.

"Two Dawson friends would be left behind: Kate and Tina. Kate told me she didn't want to go to Nome, even for a brief time. She claimed that she would leave Dawson soon anyway, to join Alex Pantages, marry, and perform in his new theaters. I never wanted to lose contact with the first friend I made on my trip to the north. Kate would always have a special place in my heart. Tina said they thought about moving to Nome, but would put off a decision until the next summer, when their baby was a few months old. Cyryl decided to go back to New York City because he hadn't the heart to continue with the business in the far North without Anya.

"Sam's boat reservations were arranged for July 17th, and the rest of us followed two weeks later. Once it was all settled we were moving, I would have been terribly disappointed if we couldn't. I was overwhelmed with what had to be done before we left. Faith and Nick understood that we had to pack, and of course, they wanted to take everything. They danced around, singing 'Goin' ta Nome, goin' ta Nome!'

"I never thought Abigail would actually leave Dawson City for Nome, after the disappointment with Lars," Rosalie exclaimed. "But I sure understand her reasons. It was the only decision she could make to keep everyone together."

Callie agreed with Rosalie, "You know, for such a young woman... she's still just twenty-two years old at this point... I was always flabbergasted how she handled her complicated life."

"Wish I had known her; I would have asked so many questions!" Rosalie said.

Callie refreshed their coffees, and continued reading the memoir.

"Etta insisted that her wedding dress should be appropriate for the frontier life in Nome, and chose no satin or silk. However, she was beautiful in robin-egg blue linen and a bonnet to match. Her hair was braided and coiled into a bun at the nape of her neck, and she carried a bouquet of flowers, fresh from Tina's garden. Even Kate teared up as the two young lovers took their vows in front of Judge Millhouse. I reserved a suite in the Dawson Hotel for the newlyweds, so they could start out with the memory of two days totally alone. Once we reached Nome, privacy would be a luxury.

"Molly, Etta and I had just about everything packed in the shop. Every crate was carefully labeled, so when they were unpacked in the new location, filling the shelves and racks would go much faster. Tom had overseen construction of the building in Nome, and Esther purchased the furnishings. I don't know why I ever hesitated about the move.

"Sam came by the cabin a few hours before his boat departed Dawson City. Etta had taken the twins into town, so we were alone. He wanted to show me a map of where he and Frank would be prospecting, about twenty miles from Nome. Etta could stay in their camp most of the time until freeze-up, but after that, Frank, Sam, and their friend Robert, would rotate between the claim and town, so each man could enjoy the comforts of a real bed and real food occasionally. We sat at the table, with the map spread out in front of us, tracing fingers up and down landmarks. Sam seemed nervous and suddenly jumped to his feet, knocking his chair over. He apologized, straightened the chair, and paced to the window. I asked him if anything was wrong, and he laughed softly. 'No,' he answered, 'just the opposite. Everything is quite right.' He was close to me then, and I could see his blue, blue eyes searching mine. It was very quiet in the room; my breathing seemed to come hard. I suddenly thought, 'Oh, no! This can't happen again!' I turned away abruptly, leaving him confused, I'm sure. He went to the table, rolled up the map, and asked if I would be at the wharf that afternoon. I told him, 'of course,' and he let himself out the door. I stood at the window, and watched him walk slowly down the hill. Abruptly, Sam turned around, walked quickly back to the door. Without knocking, he opened it to see me standing at the window, and said, 'Forgot something.' With one quick movement Sam pulled me to him, kissed me on the mouth, stepped back and left. This time when I watched him briskly walk down the hill, I had a tiny smile on my lips.

"The boat was loaded and ready to cast off into the current when I arrived at the river. Sam was bidding everyone good-bye, since our whole contingent had gathered to wish him luck. Just before he went aboard, Sam took my hand as if to shake it; instead he pulled me slightly towards him and whispered, 'I'm happy you are coming to Nome; are you?' I could only nod, and then he said, 'Hurry.' Sam pressed a small box into my palm, and dashed up the plank. By the time I opened the gift, his barge had shoved away and I couldn't see him. Sam gave me one of the delicate lapel watches from Tina's shop. It was so thoughtful and I admitted to myself I was attracted to Sam, but I would make no more mistakes. This time, I would make sure I wasn't mistaking romance for love.

"Two weeks later, our steamer left my home of three years, and the voyage downstream sped by! Faith and Nick entertained themselves by standing at the rails (while their hands were tight in ours), watching for animals on the shore or islands, and spying smoke from chimneys and campfires off in the hills and forests. I didn't take the twins ashore when the steamer stopped in the villages. I remembered so well when Jimmy caught typhoid, and I couldn't bear it if one of my children became so ill or died. When deciding what should go with us to Nome besides clothing, Etta and I packed our favorite cooking utensils, linens and blankets, and personal treasures such as photos and books. At the last minute, I made an extravagant decision to take the claw-foot table. Many were the nights I spent writing in my journal or sewing at that golden oak surface. With my eyes closed, I could still see the light brown grain marked by dark oak streaks, which hid crayon scribbles that escaped Nick's paper. Although the cabin would be securely locked when we left, I worried that someone might break in and steal it before I decided what I would do with the contents. There was always a chance we might come back. Mother was disappointed, of course, when she received my letter telling her I would not be home that year.

"The *Willamette Belle* was carrying about one hundred souls and several tons of cargo; some travelers were going back to Seattle and points east, but most were headed for Nome. Molly shared a stateroom with me and the children; Frank and Etta had their own tiny room next door. Many evenings we all sat on deck chairs, taking in the scope of our adventure. This was Frank's first trip on this end of the Yukon, since he and Sam came into Dawson over the ice at Skagway and down from Lake Bennett. The voyage that Molly and I shared while onboard the *Aleutian Storm* through Dutch Harbor, and plowing up the strong Yukon River current to Dawson, felt like ten years in the past.

"Etta stopped wearing the last of her Indian clothing; no more moccasins, and her hair was always styled fashionably. Dressed as an Anglo woman, many would assume she was from a French-Canadian family. Leaving Dawson gave her a chance to assimilate into a world where she, and any children they might have, could avoid half-breed treatment. In Dawson our small circle of friends accepted Etta as just a friend, without reservations. However, the public at-large had a dim view of Indian women, and of men who married them. It was alright to keep an Indian girl in your cabin for the long winter nights, but unacceptable to have a legal bond.

"The voyage downstream went so much faster, and we were in Nome within two weeks of departure. Since the sea was so shallow along the coast, our ship had to anchor miles offshore so tugboats towing barges could fetch us. There were no wharfs along the beach; the barge simply took a wave upon the sand, and we were there! The narrow gangplank off the boat guided the passengers onto a filthy beach, scattered with garbage, human and animal filth, and even a bloated horse carcass. One whiff and all the women untucked hand-kerchiefs to cover their noses! Frank was attending to our baggage and cargo, so Etta and I each picked up a child and hurriedly steered through the crowd. Suddenly, Sam was at my side, guiding our group to an old flat-bed wagon. He returned to the boat, and helped Frank haul the crates and baggage, so soon we were all aboard, perched atop the boxes. We learned that the main road was named Front Street, just like Dawson's waterfront street. Tents made up the majority of 'buildings.' Many tents housed saloons and gambling halls, and there were dozens of garishly dressed women right on the street! Sam tried to hurry the horses along the muddy track, but the wagon wheels kept getting sucked into deep ruts, making the poor animals' job even harder. Sam drove the wagon down a street farther away from the beach, to Molly's new home and business: a real two-story, wood building, which housed the shop on the main floor and a large apart-ment upstairs. Esther and Tom were waiting on the porch, and swept us into their arms. Oh, how wonderful it was to be with everyone again! Tom helped move our things into the apartment, which was beautifully furnished; Esther outdid herself. A room off the back of the main level was furnished as a bedroom for when Etta or the men came into town. Tom and Esther had a home nearer the center of town, close to his warehouse and wagon yard.

"Esther's little boy was a chubby darling; they named him Thomas Langdon Doaks, after his daddy. Later we went to their house, where the Robertsons waited with some of Ida's fabulous dishes for the dinner she and Esther arranged as a celebration. It was so good to see Ida and John! Their boot business was already successful in Nome, and they had just moved into a small house behind their shop. Esther had a piano in her parlor so after dinner she played and we all sang, which prompted Faith and Nick to dance and twirl across the floor. I loved watching them try to dance jigs along with Frank and Sam; those Collins cousins kept everyone laughing and clapping. We returned to our apartment late that night, with two sleepy children who were carried upstairs by Sam, one on each shoulder. I don't know when I had ever been so happy. Sam and I lingered by the door and I remembered to thank him for the watch, which he noticed I was wearing. He leaned over and kissed me lightly on the cheek before closing the door. I was left with something sweet to dream about.

"Sam departed for the diggings by horseback the next morning. They seldom left just one man to work and guard their diggings. Robert Meyer, their partner, believed they were close to finding the mother lode at this new site off Dexter Creek, which kept tantalizing them with small, occasional nuggets. That's what all prospectors said, but I didn't dash their hopes. Frank and Etta left with the wagon bed full of supplies; twenty miles from Nome, the rough track ended, and then they had to haul everything on horseback … or men's backs, two more miles. According to Sam, the cabin wasn't any bigger than a bedroom in our new apartment, but I had no doubt that Etta would soon have it ship-shape, clean as a soapy dish. We wouldn't see any of them again until mid-October.

"Etta and I had spent only a handful of days apart since October of 1898, and I missed her terribly. Of course, she had Frank with her, but I knew for sure she missed Faith and Nick.

"While Molly and I worked day and night to get ready for a grand opening, the streets of Nome became ghostly deserted, save for a few prospectors straggling around town. Ships were anchored offshore, forbidden to unload their human cargo, since Nome had been placed under quarantine. Doctors warned that Nome had twenty-six cases of small pox, and the numbers would surely rise. No one was allowed to board a ship to leave Nome, which had hundreds of frightened people up in arms. The army posted soldiers along the waterfront to keep watch for any attempts to come or go. While most of our small group of friends had been inoculated against the pox, we stayed in our homes as much as possible, or stole from place to place under wraps. I used Molly's horse and buggy to keep the children and me from coming into contact with strangers. Faith, Nick and Tom's inoculations had been done so recently, the dr. warned against taking a chance. Tom was still running his teamster business, but he stayed in the warehouse and collected his meals from the kitchen door. Ethel and Tom would take no chances on infecting their baby boy. Tom stopped at the claim to warn everyone there, so we wouldn't see any of them for awhile longer. Etta had not been inoculated yet, so she kept close to their cabin. I was worried about my children, of course; they didn't understand why we couldn't walk down to see the Robertsons, where they always got a cookie.

During that time Molly and I arranged and rearranged the shop, preparing for our grand opening when the small pox scare was over."

November 1, 1901
Nome, Alaska Territory

Dear Alice,

If Dawson is "Paris of the North", Nome is "Calcutta of the West". A shoddier, dirtier settlement, full of outlaws and shysters, couldn't be found elsewhere on the west coast of the U.S. Perhaps San Francisco went through the same growing pains before it became the grand city of today, but my imagination can't stretch far enough for Nome to approach that level of civilization. I suppose I should remember that my first impression of Dawson was that it smelled terribly and had unsavory characters wandering the streets. And like Dawson, Nome has some very nice townspeople. The native people in this part of Alaska are Eskimos, instead of Indians found in the Klondike. Eskimos are sadly more primitive, caused by living in such a forbidding place along the coast, without many resources. I am amazed they manage to survive on this hostile ledge of existence.

I am enclosing a map to show you where I have been in the Yukon and Alaska Territories these last few years.

Right away when we arrived, Nome had a small pox scare, and the whole town was under quarantine. I was frantic with worry about Faith and Nicholas, but we came through alright. For over three weeks, we dared not venture out, but thank goodness, the epidemic was not as severe as the doctors feared.

Maison de Mode had a successful grand opening! Women in town are so happy to buy clothes that fit perfectly, in the latest styles. Now that Etta is back in Nome for the winter, we can take more clients. Molly and Esther are as happy as they can be, back together again. Esther can't spend a lot of her time sewing, with the baby's demands, but we still see her almost every day. The children have outgrown almost everything, so Etta and I sew into the nights on new wardrobes for them. We agree that they shouldn't be dressed in like fabric and colors, since each child is his or her own person.

Each of our friends at the diggings comes to town for a few days every month. Right now all they can do out there is to thaw the frozen permafrost, just like on the Klondike claims. The difference between these inland claims and those on the beaches is the lack of water available for the clean up later, so it has to be done quickly when snow starts melting. Ditches are going to be dug starting next summer, to bring more water into the gulch. Frank just left to go back to Dexter Creek, so Sam should show up in a few days. Samuel Collins is nothing like any other man I've known. His mind seems perpetually at work, whether he is digging a hole or discussing a book. We have energetic conversations regarding Nome's future, corrupt government men, the weather, raising children, and women's roles in life. On the latter, he is quite liberal and believes that every state should allow women to vote; I certainly agree with him! Sam's looks are nice, better than average I think. He is rather tall, but not too much, and wears his dark hair short. A clean shaven face reveals one small scar on a cheek. Perhaps I will ask how he got that. But I often remind myself that men don't always reveal their true personalities to women, until it's too late.

We see many of Dawson's notorious people around Nome, like Tex Rickard, a saloon keeper. I think he lost his saloon in a card game. Nome hasn't an opera house yet, nor a theater; just small, shabby tents with false fronts, emitting tinny piano tunes and screeching laughter from saloon girls. A 'red light district' is located behind a board fence just off Front Street, and women who work there seldom leave those confines, I'm told. Back in Oregon, I could not even hint I knew of such things.

A newspaper, The Nome Nugget, is published once a week, with news of Seattle and points beyond. During the winter, our mail has to travel by dog sled thru Unalakleet, then on frozen rivers to the outside. I'm told that a letter can take two months to reach its destination; the same applies to mail coming into Nome.

Don't faint, but I am thinking of making a visit to Oregon next summer, perhaps to stay. Don't mention it to Mother if you see or write her. I want to show off my darling children as they are truly my proudest accomplishment. Before our first snowfall, I took Nicholas and Faith out on the tundra for a last romp in the grass, where the clean smell of the hills clears my head. It's actually very pretty here, away from town.

Your best friend,
Abigail

"By next summer she will have been gone… what… four years? A lot of water has flowed under the bridge!" Ray said. "I'll bet she had trouble adjusting to a different kind of life back here."

Callie nodded, "Ray, it's interesting that you thought of that. When she finally did get back to Oregon, Abby appreciated things like easier travel, faster communication, and better medical care. But after those years in the quiet North, she couldn't think of living in a city."

"Hearing her comments to Alice about Sam, I'm curious whether this friendship blossomed. I think she'd have had to overcome how she felt about the mistakes she'd made with Lars and the sergeant, before trusting another man," Rosalie said, raising her eyebrows.

"Celebrating Christmas and the 1902 New Year was made even better when Robert offered to stay at the diggings through the holidays, so our families could be together. When he came to town two weeks later, we surprised him with his favorite dinner of liver and onions, mashed potatoes, gravy, and a large fruit cobbler. Robert kept a string of sled dogs so Frank and Sam learned to handle the team for their trips to town.

"I saw Mr. Holder at the bank and he told me his wife had not returned to the North, which was good news to me. He didn't seem to mind it very much, either.

"Almost every week, someone organized a dance or fancy ball; when Frank was in town, he proudly took Etta, and they danced until dawn! She was so happy, more talkative in public, just plain more sure of herself. Her confidence had risen, and mine had declined. During the day I enjoy visiting with customers, being spontaneous and engaged. Faith and Nick usually played around me when I was in the shop's sewing room, but when they got too restless, Etta and I bundled them up until just their eyes showed, and took them to see Aunty Esther. They were learning their letters and numbers, and loved to listen to me read their favorite stories. However, once the twins and Molly were asleep, and Etta said goodnight, I was left with just my doubts and uncertainties. Sometimes I had a nip of cherry cordial when I couldn't sleep.

"When Sam was in Nome, he wanted to go to a New Years Eve dance with Frank and Etta; however, he needed a dance partner! I agreed to go, if he promised we wouldn't stay very long. Sam was quite a good dancer, and even surprised me with sweeping waltzes and fast two-steps. The band consisted of two fiddles, a flute and an accordion, but the crowd couldn't have been happier with a full orchestra! Frank and Sam treated everyone with an Irish Jig, which made Tom's warehouse almost vibrate from the crowd's roaring approval. The huge iron pot belly stove Tom brought in to keep the temperature above freezing was adequate, since most everyone danced to keep warm, and those who didn't, kept themselves wrapped in furs. Many flaring skirts showed red long johns underneath, and short sleeved dresses exposed arms covered by woolen or quilted underwear. Not even forty below zero outside could dampen the crowd's enthusiasm.

"I was always so proud to be seen with Sam, since he was well regarded among men and women and quite handsome too. Sam had little weather crinkles at the corners of his eyes, a straight nose, and a firm mouth that was prone to produce a shy smile. His hands, which had been smooth in Dawson, were callused after working at the claim. His fingers were long, perfect for playing the piano, and later I discovered that he was quite good at exactly that. The thing I most admired about Sam was his mind, and his desire to push the boundaries of known theories. I observed how he inspired younger people to stretch their minds to the limit, and discouraged them from becoming too comfortable with an idea before trying to improve it. He admitted that being in the classroom was what he enjoyed the most.

"Sam and I left the festivities at midnight, not able to talk until we reached the shop. He slept on a pallet in the sewing area, to give Etta and Frank privacy in the extra room. I thanked Sam for such a nice evening, and he started to help me remove my long face scarf. It was caught on a hair comb, so he finally had to remove the comb to prevent the yarn from unraveling. A long lock of hair fell to my shoulder, which Sam curled around his fingers while staying very close to me. My knees felt weak, like water had replaced my bones. Sam's fingers moved from the curl, up the side of my face, and tenderly touched my lips with his fingertips. I couldn't keep my hands from touching his face, and I imagined running my fingers through his hair. His kiss was soft and brief, tender and shaky, and then he rested his forehead on mine. I wanted more, and knew he did too. Looking into my eyes, Sam said, 'Dear girl.' I shifted my eyes away, and said 'Sam. I …' He stopped me with another kiss, this time not so brief or soft. His arms pulled me closer until I felt I would faint. Sam leaned back, finally, and said, 'Not to worry, Abby. Until I have something to offer, something you deserve, we'll take our time.' I couldn't hide that I enjoyed the kiss; in fact, I was totally involved and he knew it. Sam seemed so sure of his feelings for me, but I remembered that I accepted Barrett's proposal because he was sure. I had to be sure this time. The way he called me Abby, picking up Etta's nickname for me, was sweetly endearing, and I thought about that and the kiss far into the night.

"John Robertson mentioned to me when we first arrived in Nome that he was a member of the new Nome School Board. He knew that I taught school in Oregon, and asked if I would consider teaching the youngest primary students in the Bridge School this spring. The former teacher was ill with frostbit lungs, so they needed a local replacement before one could be recruited from outside. I had to talk to Molly, of course, but she assured me that since Etta was working until she returned to the diggings in May, the shop could get along alright. My teaching job also meant that Etta and Molly would have to watch the children during the day, but Esther offered to help with that. I was so excited about teaching again! Schools were closed until the weather broke, and the daytime temperature reached at least 25 degrees below zero. I couldn't wait to tell Sam; I knew he would be pleased.

"A letter from Kate arrived telling me she was finally leaving Dawson, probably soon over the ice, heading to Los Angeles where Alex Pantages lived. Although she had given him a small fortune over the last several months, Kate was taking several thousand dollars of Klondike gold with her. I was glad she would finally have a more legitimate venue for her acting talents. Etta, Molly and I read her letter together, and agreed that it was rather sad. Kate sounded very insecure and had always worried about Alex's commitment to her; however, she still wanted to marry him.

"It remained so very cold outside and sometimes inside too. That country was so different from the Klondike; a miner up the Yukon River could feed himself by killing a moose or caribou, grow potatoes in the summer, and graze his horse on the slopes of nearby hills. He could build his own cabin from trees in the forests, and burn wood in his stove to cook on and heat the cabin. The Seward Peninsula where the new city of Nome had emerged was a vast barren stretch of land, where no large game was left. Aside from a few reindeer imported to teach the natives about herding, there was nothing to hunt that supplied red meat. Various kinds of fish were available in the local rivers and lakes, which Eskimos eagerly sold when they had a surplus. They used nets to catch ptarmigan all year; ducks and geese added to the food supply when they migrated back. Virtually all food except those few fowl and fish had to be purchased and shipped from Seattle. Lumber sold for a premium price in Nome, since there were no trees and all the beach driftwood was used up by earlier prospectors. Logs and lumber were shipped from Juneau or Puget Sound. Heating cabins and businesses was more costly since fuel, such as coal and petroleum had to be bought; all of this was shipped in before the ocean locked up with sheets of ice and beaches froze solid for miles. Not so many cheechakoes stayed for a winter, unless they had found enough gold to carry them through the eight months of dormancy. Frank and Sam knew all this, and were wise to plan and save. Sam confided that they had enough to last through next summer without a good strike. Few laborers' jobs in town paid enough to support a man all winter. My teacher's pay was less than what I made working for Molly, but I had enough saved so the children and I could live for two or three years in Nome, even at the high prices. The money set aside in Prineville wouldn't be touched until I returned to Oregon. Sam, Frank, and Robert just had to make a strike that summer!

"By February, the weather warmed up ... to twenty below zero! School finally began and I'll admit that I was a bit scared. The school had few books, so I was proud to unpack the copies of Appleton's First Reader I took to Dawson for the church school. Most of my students were children of merchants or government men. Eskimo children were not allowed to attend the public schools in Nome, but there were no other schools for them. In Oregon we had Indian schools, on and off reservations, many of which were boarding schools. I didn't understand why Eskimo and Indian children were not allowed to attend with whites when no school just for them was established. Sometimes the missions helped educate those indigenous children, but nothing was available in Nome. I'd heard civic leaders complain that 'those' children were not capable of learning much beyond drying fish and harvesting seal oil. Indeed, the practice of coating their hair with oil caused Eskimos of the Seward Peninsula to smell rancid, and when combined with their ignorance of soap and water, it tended to shock a person's sense of smell. But I had seen what education could do; my friend Moses was as bright and clean as anyone I knew, all because of education. Etta was guided by her mother, who lived with a white man long enough to realize she had to make sure her daughters moved into the modern world of opportunities. I liked to think I had something to do with Etta's continued progress, since she soon read as well as I, and would never have endorsed following ancient ways. There was a tinge of guilt sometimes when we talked about her Indian half's culture and traditions. Etta mentioned once that going the way of the whites had cut half of her away. I owed her everything, and reassured her that some of those traditions were worth keeping.

"My ten primary students in first and second grades included just two girls, who were cousins. They came to school dressed like catalog models, with their hair in ringlets and carrying patent leather shoes to wear once they were inside the schoolhouse. The boys could be rowdy when turned loose; however, a stern reminder of where they were usually brought them to order. One of my first grade boys was Jimmy Doolittle, who was small for his age and the quietest child in the whole class. He came to school early some days just so we could talk about what he liked, such as handstands and shooting marbles.

"There wasn't much difference in teaching in Nome from teaching in Prineville: I just had to build a bigger fire in the stove each day! I was so busy all day, that I didn't have time to think about how much I missed Faith and Nick; it was only when I started tramping home, that I felt like I hadn't seen them for a week!

"Bridge School was on one end of town, and Molly's place was on the opposite end, so my route passed the many dozens of shops and offices for a variety of goods and services: groceries, doctors, mining supplies, dentists, lawyers, barbers, clothing, harnesses, fuel, restaurants, rooming houses and hotels, the same you would find in an average town outside except Nome also had many saloons. Since the afternoons were dark when I left the school, lights from all the businesses guided me through the streets. Tom usually gave me a ride in the mornings on his way to the warehouse."

"Say, is that the same Jimmy Doolittle of World War II fame?" Ray blurted.

"Oh, he sure is!" Callie responded. "Grandma Abby always told me that he was her favorite! She was still alive when he made that Tokyo raid, and bragged to everyone how she taught him in first grade."

"I don't suppose you are going to give us a hint of how long she taught in Nome!" Rosalie guessed.

"Well, that would spoil the story! I will tell you this: she never accepted the rule about Eskimo children not being allowed to go to

149

school with whites. Abby had a soft spot for those kids, you know. She was a stickler for fairness, all of her life. Alice didn't feel the same way about Indians; Oregon provided schools for them, but Abby felt it was unfair to take the children away from families and send them to boarding schools. The two women just didn't talk about that, or politics. Ray, do you want to read awhile?" Callie asked, as she handed the memoir to him.

XIII

· ·

"OUR HOUSEHOLD OF THREE WOMEN AND TWO children seemed to always be anxiously waiting for a visit from the men at the diggings. Frank always stayed a week, but Sam and Robert were in town just a few days. Sam said they found a little more 'color' in some thawed gravel forty feet farther along the gulch, so their spirits were up. They wouldn't really know much until the clean up in late spring. The men began speaking of their claim as the Missouri Mine, after Robert's home state.

"Sam prodded me into learning how to drive a dog team! After only two lessons, I really knew very little, but at least I could drive the dogs a block or two without tangling the traces. Nick was crazy about riding in the basket, and screamed, 'Faster, Sam, faster!' Faith would ride only if we promised to drive slowly, and not bump too much.

"Before Sam came into town in March, I made myself a new wool dress; the fabric was a plaid design in gold and brown. I used plain off-white wool to trim the long sleeves and stand up collar. I knew Sam would ask me out to dinner; having him proud of the way I looked was important to me. We talked all through dinner, dessert, and coffee; he excitedly told me about the claim and its possibilities, and I prattled on about the twins and my teaching position. Sam was an incredible listener, tilting his head when I spoke as if he was making sure he could hear every word. Sometimes he was so intense

I would feel my face get hot under his gaze. Our attraction to each other was apparent, but cautious. Sam made me so proud to be teaching in Nome; when school was dismissed for the day, he would pull up at the door with his dog team, so I could drive it home. Once my team met another on Front Street, who didn't like the looks of each other; an immense tangle of snarling dogs erupted. The other musher snapped at me for being a 'blank-blank woman, trying to be like a man.' Sam used the same tactic on that man as he used on the dogs: grabbed him by the collar and threw him aside. After forcing the man to apologize, Sam motioned for me to take my place back on the runners; he trotted along beside me the rest of the way home. I couldn't keep from hugging Sam tightly when we stopped in front of the shop, and gave him a peck on the cheek which he accepted without complaint.

Tina wrote that she had a new baby girl named Anya, but the letter took almost three months to arrive. I had a feeling Tina would name a girl after her best friend. I wondered about their plans to move to Nome that summer.

"In April a letter from Mother had surprising news! She was going to marry Mr. Carter! She sounded like a young girl with her first beau, and I cried with happiness when I told Etta. Emily had excelled at the university and would be home for the June wedding. Mother wanted me there too, of course; I would've had to leave over the ice right then, since Nome was iced in for another six weeks. I couldn't go for a number of reasons.

"It was so much fun to watch Etta and Frank, sweetly nudging each other when we were sitting at Molly's huge dining table. Etta made several friends in Nome, young married women who had husbands working on claims. She and I joined a book club that met once a month at the Methodist Church; our selection that April was

Washington Square by Henry James. It's a book full of anxiety and betrayal and was hard for me to read, since I identified with some parts. Our next selection was *Sense and Sensibility* by Jane Austen, which I'd already read, and absolutely loved.

"When there was only one more month until the end of school, I couldn't believe the time had passed so quickly. My time with the students had been so good for me, and I think I made a difference, being their teacher. I hoped I could teach again the next fall, but that was a long time away.

"The gulch where the men were prospecting started to thaw in May, so they moved farther down the streambed to try a new hole. Etta went back to their cabin that week and threw the men out while she scrubbed and cleaned. Sam came into town then, bought new work clothes and replaced some tools. We attended a spring dance, watched the orange sun flirt with the horizon, and kissed in the twilight. I told Molly that I thought I was in love with Sam, but I had been wrong before.

"Just after Sam returned to the claim, Tom Doaks was gravely injured by a runaway wagon. While he was in the Nome Hospital, Esther wouldn't leave his side, so we all took care of the baby, inbetween feedings. Robert was in town when it happened, and left immediately for the claim to bring Etta back, since we all knew she would want to help. Tom seemed to rally some days, but the broken bones and internal injuries from being pinned underneath the heavy wagon, were too severe to survive. We prayed for his recovery; however, he died the 10th of May.

"Tom's funeral was attended by almost the whole town; he was such a friend to so many. I, for one, would never forget his kindness after Barrett died. Esther managed to make the arrangements, and forced herself through the day, but Molly knew she was near collapsing. Esther finally slept that evening, with some help of laudanum from the doctor. She tearfully told us she would not live in the house Tom built, so we had her and little Tommy move into our spare room; Etta and Frank stayed in Esther's house when they were in town, until it was sold. I was devastated for Esther, and my heart broke every time I saw her face so tear stained. I realized that Sam was reliving the grief he felt when his wife and child died, because he was so quiet, and remained a shadowy figure when he was in Nome for the funeral. The men left immediately afterwards, so I had no chance to speak with him for awhile.

"School ended for the year and many of the students had to help their families with mining activities running full bore, and shops busy preparing for the arrival of the first ships. Molly and I tried to keep our minds on millinery customers, and new fabrics. We hoped to tempt Esther to rejoin our sewing circle.

"The twins grew so much that year that I had to admit they weren't babies any longer. Nick loved to draw, and used his crayons down to the nub. He would sit at the claw-foot table for hours, copying animals from a new book about plants and animals that Mother sent. Faith wanted to be a ballerina, at least at that particular time! The previous month she declared she would be a teacher like Mommy. It was important to me for them to be anything they desired. In June of that year, an astonishing event occurred which insured I would always be able to provide a secure future for my sweet children.

"Mr. Holder sent a message to Maison de Mode asking me to come to the bank, and I couldn't imagine what he wanted. He began by saying that he had received a letter from the Royal Mounted Police Commissioner in Dawson City, about a recent discovery. Some Indian fishermen tried to pull an old fishing net out of a thawing oxbow along the Yukon River, when they found it was snagged on something. When it was finally dragged to shore, a battered canoe was tangled in the net. The men found two canvas bags of gold tied into the canoe; they were marked with the bank's name like the ones my mine foreman used for the bank deposits. Since the discovery was located just downstream from where the two thieves' bodies were found, the Mounties determined the gold was from the Black Dog! I could hardly believe it! As exciting as this news was, I asked for Mr. Holder's confidentiality, and told no one at that time. I knew that my close friends would be so happy, but I worried that Sam would think he had to compete with me in finding a fortune. Mr. Holder handled a transfer of the funds … almost $15,000 … to my account in Prineville. He suggested that a reward would be appropriate for the men who turned in the bags of gold to authorities, and I agreed.

"I had such a strange feeling about this news; as a bride-to-be four years earlier, I was never on the quest for gold, unlike most of the masses moving north. Here I was, with a small fortune in my name, without having suffered the hardships common to prospectors. Thousands of gold seekers risked their lives and persevered through terrible ordeals, only to return home broke and broken. Many never returned home, forever following the next rumor. I saw those men in Dawson and Nome; families lost contact with husbands, brothers, and fathers, never sure whether they were dead or alive. And I had a small fortune, without lifting a pick or shovel."

"Tell me, Callie, she says her fortune was about $15,000; how much is that equal to now?" Rosalie asked.

"It was like winning a $400,000 lottery today!" Callie quipped. "Grandma Abigail considered that money a gift, and made a point of using it wisely. Not very many people ever knew about it."

"A letter from Kate brought distressing news of her situation. Pantages married a young socialite in San Francisco, and the money Kate sent to him was all spent on the two-timing scoundrel's theaters, with only his name on the deeds. She was devastated, of course, about his betrayal; in addition, most of the money she made for her retirement was gone. Thank goodness Kate was astute enough to hold back some of those gold nuggets thrown at her feet that last winter. She joined a vaudeville circuit that booked shows throughout the west and got top billing as the 'Real Klondike Kate.' We had held out hope that Kate would make money on her theater investments, but personally, Pantages never had her wellbeing in mind. I made a promise to myself back then in 1902 that I would see Kate again.

"Our men at the claim seldom came into town; they were that busy digging and washing the dirt. Etta did make trips to Nome more often since she couldn't stay away from the children very long. And they certainly missed her, always asking, 'Can we go see Aunty Etta?'"

"Didn't Klondike Kate end up in Oregon?" Rosalie asked.

"I'm thinking about dishing up some new-fangled ice cream I bought at that new Goody's shop. It's a chocolate almond flavor… want some?"

Both Rosalie and Ray nodded, and soon everyone was scraping their bowls and making satisfied sounds. However, Rosalie noted that Callie hadn't answered her question about Kate.

"At last it happened!! Gold!! Etta, Molly, Esther and I were at work in the sewing room when Frank rode in like a Plains Indian, jumped off his horse and burst into the shop! He picked Etta up, twirled her around, and yelled, "We found it! We're in the gold!" And then he took a poke from his vest pocket, poured the contents onto the cutting table, and we three gasped in unison. Nuggets! Nuggets the size of pecans and a few larger than that! Frank says it happened all of a sudden; after almost a year of being teased by a few tiny nuggets here and there, Sam's shovel exposed a treasure hole full of gold! Since Frank had been in a hurry to tell us the news, he hadn't brought the wagon to town. While he arranged to borrow a wagon and pick up supplies, we all packed our things for a few days stay at the Missouri Mine. Everyone went except Esther, who offered to take care of the shop for Molly."

Ray exclaimed, "I can't believe they actually struck gold!"

"They could hardly believe it themselves," Callie said. "Grandma Abby told me that they were almost delirious with excitement, wondering just how much gold would be found. And of course she couldn't wait to see Sam."

"Frank bought a large tent which became the bedroom for women and children at the claim. We stayed a week, and dreaded coming home. Sam and Robert clearly needed a rest by the time we arrived, so they hired two men who were wandering along the gulch, looking for work. These men were put on the shovel brigade, while Frank washed and filtered the gold from dirt piled in the hopper of a rocker. It was much the same process used at the Black Dog Mine, and reminded me of the weeks I spent working there. I worked alongside Frank, and then Sam, scraping small flakes of gold from the riffles at the bottom of the rocker. The bigger nuggets were easy to pick out by hand, and we were absolutely giddy. Our days were long, and since summer solstice was close, a dusky twilight was as dark as it got. Etta and Molly kept track of the children, and made sure hot food was readily available on the cabin's small stove. Faith and Nick played in the dirt and rocks around the claim, pretending to find gold nuggets of their own. We all were covered with grime by bedtime; washing before we crawled under covers seemed the right thing to do, but with just a bucket of water and a cloth, getting clean was just a few degrees better than dirty.

"Faith and Nick celebrated their third birthday near the Arctic Circle, surrounded by gold nuggets and a lopsided cake. Men from surrounding claims dropped by and soon we had fiddle music and dancing. I appreciated that no one became drunk to ruin the evening, but it seemed like these men associated my children with the ones they left behind. It was a birthday party they might not remember, but I would. After the guests left for their own claims, and the children were asleep, I decided that it was a perfect time to tell everyone about my recovered gold. Since Frank worked for me at the mine, he knew about the theft, and had told Sam. All my friends were happy to hear justice was done, although the recovery was almost unbelievable. Later, Sam and I talked about it, and I apologized for keeping it to myself; he said he would have probably done the same thing.

"The evening before Molly, the children and I left, Sam and I sat alone on the hilltop above the claim, watching the orange sun attempting to set; after a struggle, it suddenly dipped behind the hills, only to pop up a short time later. This 'Land of the Midnight Sun' was certainly a place of wonder, when you ignored the hardships. We could see to our north a great cloud of dust, stirred by machinery working claims to retrieve gold left behind by other means. Sam said that within a few years, every inch of soil around Nome would be churned several times; of course, history proved he was right. I asked what he planned to do with his share of the gold, and he chuckled, saying, 'I've been too tired to think about it recently, but during the winter I dreamed of big trees surrounding a large white house, and a lawn to mow! And I'd like to have fresh eggs every day!' I laughed and had to agree. He took my hands between his, and kissed them tenderly...oh, I melted. With that small gesture, my heart beat faster, and I felt that Sam would protect me always. I hadn't had that feeling in a long time. I wanted to tell Sam everything about mistakes I'd made in the last four years, but I was afraid. He leaned over and held my chin for a breathtaking kiss, one that I wished would never end. He finally said to me, 'Abby, we have a lot to talk about when I'm not tired and dirty.' I could only nod. Sam asked whether I still planned to take the children to Oregon this summer. I hadn't really decided until just before we heard about the strike. One of the school board members asked if I wanted to teach a class of third-graders that fall, and I told him I would. It was the perfect excuse for staying in Nome. Sam couldn't hide how pleased he was. I dreaded writing Mother and Emily, but I just couldn't leave right then.

"For the next few weeks I hardly had time to breathe. Maison de Mode was buried in dress and hat orders; so much so that Molly hired two seamstresses who had just arrived by steamship. Esther and baby Tommy left the next week, after she received a letter from her brother in Idaho asking her to accept an offer to live with his family. The North hadn't been the same for Esther since Tom's death, and I felt she wouldn't stay into the winter. Molly, Esther and I had been through so much together, all the way from Seattle as cheechakoes, that it was hard to imagine her living so far away. Tina and Jozef decided to stay in Dawson another year, then move back to New York; they wanted to own an art gallery in Manhattan, and would soon have enough saved to finance that dream. Our clan, which was so close in Dawson, was breaking apart, but I had to accept that it was the nature of things.

"There was something afoot with Molly, and that something was Robert. When we were at the mine after the strike, I noticed he spent a lot of time walking in and out of the cooking cabin; then when he took a rest in the evenings, he and Molly would sit by the tent on upturned barrels, and chat for an hour or two. When we returned to Nome, Robert often found excuses to come to town, and always planned it so he was there overnight. I'd noticed that Ida visited the shop most afternoons for tea upstairs with Molly; I decided that Molly enjoyed sharing her feelings with Ida, since they were almost the same age. Robert was in his 50's and a widower with a farm in Missouri. His daughter was married and they lived in the same area. He came to Dawson in '99 and met Sam and Frank soon after. He liked and trusted the 'boys', and always planned on the three of them being a team. I have to say that I liked him from the first, and obviously Molly did too. Etta said she knew Robert was interested in Molly, since he often asked her little things, like what Molly's favorite color was. Why was it so simple for other people to meet, fall in love, and marry? I wondered at that time if it were my fault that these things were so complicated for me.

"Etta and Frank thought they had a secret from the rest of us, and we didn't spoil their surprise, which was revealed in good time. Molly told Etta she was putting on weight, to which Etta replied 'I must be eating too many donuts.' I saw a slight smile on her face as she walked out of the room."

September 27, 1902
Nome, Alaska Territory

Dear Alice,

You'll never guess what happened!! Frank, Robert and Sam struck gold, a large amount of gold!! They've hired a good many men to dig a proper mine and build flumes to deliver water from the new canals, to wash gold from the dirt. Soon the water in the flumes will freeze up for the winter, so the men will just thaw dirt and remove it from the mine. However, over the last two months, each one's share of gold is substantial. I can't tell you how relieved I am for those men, after their years of waiting.

I am so happy to hear that your children are healthy, and fill your house with joy, just as mine do for me. I could never imagine life without Faith and Nicholas, although some days they do wear me out! My friend Etta, and her husband Frank, are expecting a baby in February; she has been such an incredible "Aunty" to my children, I have no doubt Etta will be a wonderful mother.

Sam and I don't see each other very often now, since the mine keeps him away from Nome. I am teaching a class of third graders this fall, so I haven't the time to ride out there. I do think I'm in love with him, but I must be sure that my thumping heart has less to do with anticipation of a kiss, and more to do with deep affection. I've heard that two people can have a special chemistry between them: is that love? I am very confused and don't completely trust my judgment.

Alice, you must write me all about your railroad journey to New York City, as soon as you get back. It's wonderful that you have Russ's family there to take care of the boys while you two visit all the sights. Once Faith and Nick reach school age, I must take them to see a different kind of world than what they are exposed to in the Arctic. Books are wonderful for describing deserts, skyscrapers, elephants, trolleys, and carousels; however, actually getting pricked by a cactus or riding an elevator in a tall building replaces any assumption that the pictures are just a fantasy.

Our book club is reading *Jane Eyre* by Charlotte Bronte. Have you read it yet?

A real telephone system has been installed up and down many streets in Nome, and the shop was one of the first businesses to get a line connected. It's marvelous!

By now you know I have decided to stay another winter in Nome. I think in the future I should not even mention going back to Oregon, until I am on the boat!

Your best friend,

Abigail

"I was trimming a hat one morning that October, concentrating on matching silk fabric with feathers and ribbon, when I heard the little bell over the shop door tinkle. Etta was decorating the front window of the shop, so I knew she would greet the customer, and I continued my work. Having not heard any conversation after a moment, I looked toward the sewing room doorway, and stared in disbelief. Lars was standing there, with Etta right behind him. He was dressed in a full length beaver dress coat, holding a matching fur hat, and wore fur trimmed knee-high boots. He came closer, and said, 'You're looking well, Abigail.' I could see a large diamond stud in his cravat, and an immense diamond ring. Lars noticed how I surveyed his attire, and said, 'Yes, I have done well since I last saw you.' Etta was still standing in the doorway, most likely waiting for me to ask him to leave. Suddenly, I thought, 'I'll not let him know how devastated I was when I heard he was married,' so I calmly asked, 'How is Jimmy; is he with you?' Lars replied that Jimmy was not in Nome; he was attending a military school in California. 'And how is your wife?' I inquired. Lars said she didn't like the North, and remained at their estate in Sacramento.

Impatiently, Etta interrupted, 'Abby, it's almost time for Mrs. Reynolds to arrive for her fitting.' I knew she wasn't coming until the afternoon, but looked at my lapel watch, and thanked her for reminding me. Lars apologized for interrupting my work, and asked if he could see me later; I told him I was very busy, but we could meet for dinner around seven o'clock. We agreed on a restaurant, and he left. Etta scolded me for seeing Lars at all, and I explained that I didn't want him to try to see the children, so perhaps the one meeting would satisfy him.

"After our brief meeting that night, I understood clearly what Lars thought of our affair. I told Etta and Molly what Lars had in mind and it's almost too unbearable to put on paper. He felt the need to explain that by the time Myra was out of his life, he already owned shares in several successful mining ventures. Lars said he had married his new wife because of her father's influence. Coupled with his new wealth, this connection could open doors for his political career. He always meant to see me again, to recover what we had between us in earlier days. Lars had the nerve to say that he loved only me, and wanted to take care of me and my children. He reached into his coat pocket and brought out a bundle of money, saying that he hadn't forgotten he owed Molly and me for the grubstake when he left Dawson. He laid the cash on the table and put his hand on top of mine saying, 'I hope you will seriously consider what I am offering.' I said, 'You mean you want me as your mistress.' He nodded, and replied that I would have a life of privilege, and could live anywhere I wanted. His business interests required that he travel across the U.S., so no one would be the wiser. At that moment, it was clear that I hadn't known Lars at all. I let him think I was considering the proposition, and then finally spoke, with a syrupy sweet smile on my lips. 'You must have mistaken me for someone else. I have no need of your fortune, since I have my own. You may believe that you are in love with me; however, I am certainly not in love with you. Poor Lars, I don't think you know what love is.' Lars' face went white with disbelief, then with anger. Before he could regain his voice, I rose and left him and the money behind, physically and emotionally.

"Etta could hardly contain her anger. She knew what I endured over the years, when Lars led us to believe he would marry me if he were free. Molly and Etta knew everything, and took Lars' comments personal. I reminded them we were better served by putting Lars' words behind us; my own foolish heart was at fault. That being said,

I refused to look back. I only looked at my children, asleep, without a care in the world."

Callie closed the memoir part-way, and sighed. "Grandma Abigail was actually devastated by the opinion Lars had of her, that she would become his mistress."

"Well, I think she was in love, and just lost her head. There are many women in the world who've made the same mistakes," Rosalie maintained. "He sure showed his true colors with that proposition. My opinion is that he wouldn't have suggested such a thing if he really loved Abigail."

"I always thought there was something sleazy about him," Ray said.

"Oh, you did not!" Rosalie laughed, as she kicked at Rays' foot. "We all were fooled, just like Abby."

XIV

. . . .

"ABOUT THE FIRST OF NOVEMBER, THE BERING SEA exploded in a fury of hurricane winds and waves that crashed wildly onshore for four days! Many buildings along Front Street were no longer standing afterwards, and several streets were impassable. We lost two windows from flying debris and for a time I was worried the building's roof would be torn away. Frank managed to reach town to make certain we were alright. He said the winds reached inland far enough to tear apart some of the mine's flumes, which couldn't be repaired until the next spring.

"I missed Sam the next few weeks. When I asked Frank about Sam, he just said they were concerned about thieves stealing their equipment, so Sam and Robert took shifts supervising the workers and guarding the mine. They'd built another cabin for the extra men so they wouldn't have to spend the winter in tents.

"Molly confided that Robert asked her to be his wife, and they would marry in the spring. We all thought it was wonderful they had each other at this time in their lives. Molly was a little sad that Esther wasn't in Nome to share in her happiness. Etta absolutely glowed with her condition, and Frank doted on his little wife when he was home. She fussed at us for treating her like a 'china doll', insisting that pregnancy was not an illness. Before Etta married Frank, she told him about her first child since she wanted no secrets between them. I wanted to talk to Sam, and be as honest with him.

"In the meantime, I loved teaching my young students. They asked so many questions and kept me on my toes! One day Jimmy Doolittle proudly announced to the class he had a job; the little fellow delivered issues of The Nome Nugget once a week and I praised him for his industry.

"Frank took over my dog team driving lessons when he was in town, and I became slightly more confident. I usually drove four or five dogs, but the men put all eight in harness to pull the heavy sled-full of supplies. Nick often begged to ride with me, but I wasn't quite ready to risk that!

"A new letter from Kate left me concerned, since she was dissatisfied with the circuit so far and was thinking of moving to Los Angeles. With all of her acclaim in the Klondike, Kate still seemed so unsure of herself, and I realized that perception was a result of Pantages' betrayal. Having been through the same difficulty, my heart went out to her.

"Mother wrote that the boys were happy with a man in the house, and she had become accustomed to her husband's habits. She loved him because he tried so hard to please her. Emily excelled in her classes, and had secured a place for the next summer with a team which would excavate some ruins in Utah. I was so proud of my little sister!

"I wrote Kate about Lars showing up in Nome and his proposition for me. I could imagine her reaction when she read about it! Frank said that Lars was still in Nome, but I managed to avoid him.

"A few days later Sam came into town after he heard a story from one of his workmen. The hurt in Sam's face was unmistakable when he told me the man said he saw me dining with a 'rich dandy'. On top of that, the workman saw the man hand me some money, before I walked away. It was as if someone had slapped me across the face; I couldn't speak for a moment, but realized the time had come to tell Sam everything. I had wanted to do so for a long time.

"Listening carefully, like he always did, with his head cocked to hear every word, I slowly detailed what my life was like in Prineville, and why I agreed to marry Barrett. Sam nodded occasionally, yet didn't say a word. When I told him about Lars, and how I thought I was in love, Sam stiffened and pulled back as if he was offended. Through my tears I told him all about our affair, and then how I learned Lars hadn't loved me at all. I couldn't make the words come out any more. Finally Sam said, almost in a whisper, 'It's an old story…a selfish man takes advantage of a naïve girl.' We then sat there in silence for a long time, while I wondered what Sam was thinking. Slowly, I began to realize I couldn't change who I was or what I did. I wasn't a bad person, even though I had made a big mistake. Sam was surprised when I stood and walked to the door. I said, 'That's who I am, and I think you know we are through. I will not spend the rest of my life apologizing.' I hid in Molly's bedroom, refused to see anyone, and cried the rest of the day. Etta stayed with me that night, and said Sam was called to the mine to help an injured man. He told Etta he would be back in two or three days, and had to talk to me.

"Two days later I dressed early and found Frank in the kitchen, speaking in low tones to Molly. I asked him what was wrong, and he stood there with shoulders slumped, looking sadly at the floor. At last Frank said, 'Sam is gone.' A letter from Sam's mother had arrived the previous day, asking him to come home because his father was desperately ill. That very morning, he left directly from the Missouri Mine, traveling overland by dog team to St. Michaels, and he hoped to find a way to reach an ice-free harbor to continue on to Seattle. His note to Frank said he would try to be back by spring. Sam also sent a note to me, which read, 'We are not through, no matter what you say. Yours always, Sam.' Knowing what an honorable man Sam was, I wasn't exactly comforted. He would never be able to accept my mistakes; I should never have told him. I think if I hadn't had Nick and Faith, I would've gone mad that long winter. The country was closing in on me, for the first time in four years."

"Grandma Abigail was at the lowest point in her life that winter. She didn't even write in her journal all that much. Alice seldom heard from her either. One time Grandma and I were talking about her years in Nome, and she said she would have done anything to erase the memory of that winter from her life," Callie said.

Rosalie said, "I am just so depressed myself. I would ask you to reassure us that everything turned out alright, but I know you won't disclose any details ahead of time!"

"Oh, so much happens now to Abby, you have to hear it as it plays out."

"Christmas was quiet, although we decorated the house to please the children, and attended a party held at the new school building. Mr. Holder dressed up as St. Nicholas, and later Faith kept calling her brother St. Nick, which ended when he pushed her over the hassock. They were truly two different people: Faith was a teaser and knew she was cute; Nicholas was stubborn and a perfectionist. Etta and Frank were anxious for their baby to greet the world, and had picked names: a boy would be named Henry for Frank's father, and a girl would be Sarah, the name a missionary gave Etta's mother.

"When the weather warmed up the next week, school resumed. The temperature had been almost fifty below zero for three weeks. When a door opened for someone to rush inside, the cold air hit the room's warmth, and immediately formed a cloud which hid the whole end of the room.

"On March 3, 1903, Henry Collins arrived, hale and hearty! Etta's lying-in was very brief, and she was quickly back downstairs, with her son tucked in a box beside her, or in a sling across her breast. Frank was so proud he literally 'busted his buttons.' Frank received word from Sam that his father had died. He was staying on in Colorado to help his mother with legal issues, but he hoped to be back in Nome by June.

"Molly and Robert certainly proved that love was for all ages, just like my Mother. They let all of us in on their plans to marry in May, and Molly told us more about him. When Robert's family immigrated to America from England, his name was Rhouben Meir. His father changed their names, afraid the children would not have access to schools and jobs if their Jewish origins were known. So Molly had indeed found her perfect match and would become Mrs. Robert Meyer on May 19. Robert confided to me their mine appeared to be richer than they first thought; he expected it would top many of the other mines along Dexter Creek and others in the area.

"By the middle of May ice along the beaches was mostly broken up, but still stacked like gigantic rafts just beyond Front Street. The school term ended and ships began arriving two weeks later, working their way through the shifting ice field. I almost dreaded the onslaught of newcomers since the town was so much more unruly when it was crowded. Cheechakoes landing on the frontier's shores for the first time seemed to have left all propriety back home. It was like they had just bought a license to be raucous and wild.

"The world almost brought me to my knees on a June morning, when a young woman came into the shop. She was looking for a shawl, so Molly showed her our selection. Molly introduced herself and asked if she had just come to Nome. The beautiful lady replied that her name was Careen Collins, and she had accompanied Sam Collins to Nome. She went on to say Sam had recommended the Maison de Mode as the best shop in town for clothing. He also told her he knew the owner, and a young woman working here, Abigail Rogers. Since she had met Molly, she said she hoped to meet Abigail sometime. I thought to myself how glad I was that she didn't see me in the back of the shop, and I quickly slipped into the sewing room. Molly, being the good friend she was, said I wasn't there at that time, but she would let me know. I had to sit down immediately, before I fainted, and I don't ever faint. Then I knew... Sam found someone else, or they were engaged all along. Again I wondered just how I attracted men who just wanted me temporarily.

Rosalie interrupted, "Oh, no! He got married!"

"I think he had a fiancé all along, and Abby was being duped again," Ray asserted.

"Everything was so mixed up between Sam and Abby," Rosalie added. "Maybe going back to Colorado offered him the time to think over their relationship."

Ray said, "Well, whatever the reason, he is out of her life now."

July 8, 1903
Nome, Alaska Territory

Dear Alice,

Your letter was so full of news, wonderful news! What a surprise... a new baby girl! Louise is such a pretty name; your mother must be very happy with that choice. I'm so sorry that Russ lost so many sheep this winter; I didn't realize you had such a deep snow pack. Will he replace them right away?

My dear friend Molly has married Robert Meyer, but they have postponed a honeymoon until the mining season begins to slow down in the fall.

All spring my children treated Etta's little boy, Henry, as their own plaything! Faith rocked his cradle until he slept, softly reciting her own favorite bedtime stories. Nick dangled bright objects in front of Henry, or made funny faces, just to see the baby laugh. I am sure I've seen Henry look around for the children when they were out of the room. Etta and Henry joined Frank at the mine two weeks ago, and I suspect that Henry misses the twins as much as they miss him.

Sam just returned to Nome; however, it's clear we have no future together. It's so complicated.

The Missouri Mine is already producing steadily, keeping fifteen men busy digging into the gravel, and washing out the gold. Although I don't own a share, I'm so happy for them, and especially for Etta. She is so level-headed and sensible that Frank's share has no chance of being squandered, as so often happens in these gold rush towns.

Ida and John Robertson sold their boot shop, and are leaving Nome by the end of July. Ida confessed that they have enough money set aside to take care of them the rest of their lives. As they look for a nice warm place to live, California seems to be beckoning. Nick and Faith already know that "Aunty Ida and Unka John" are leaving. I heard Faith tell Ida that we will come to see them when we move away too. I should have realized the twins understand more than I think!

No news from Kate in several months. I do wish she would write and let me know she is alright.

Nome went all-out for the Independence Day celebration, with a parade, games, costume contest, and a huge selection of food that various organizations provided! Nick wanted to dress up as a soldier, and Faith decided to be a princess (I had no doubt that's what she would choose.) They looked so cute walking in the parade with their little friends. Frank and Etta came to town on the 4th, and I'm told that Sam came in a day later. Molly decided to leave the shop under my care for a few days so she could join Robert at the mine. I think this is the first time Maison de Mode will open without her.

Mother wrote that a fire destroyed the ranch's barn, but none of the stock was lost. By now, it has probably been rebuilt, bigger and better. Emily is with her colleagues excavating Indian ruins built into a cliff, totally enamored with the process. After next year's term Emily will have earned a Bachelor's Degree; according to her last letter, and she will then pursue an advanced degree. Who would have thought, just five years ago, such things were possible in our family? Write soon,

Your best friend,

Abigail

"A few days after the celebration, after Etta and little Henry returned to the mine, Molly and I were sitting in the sewing room, enjoying our first chance in a week to talk. We heard someone come into the shop and I stepped out of the sewing room. The couple standing near the shop door turned when they heard me ask if I could help; my customers were Sam and Careen. Molly stood beside me as Sam said, 'Abigail, I don't believe you've met Careen.' The beautiful young woman held out her hand and said she had heard so much about me. I asked her what she thought of Nome, and she replied it was very different from Colorado, but she was glad she had come to see what the gold rush was like. She added that she would be returning to her home in two weeks, and was trying to talk Sam into going back with her. I was so nervous, afraid I would actually cry in front of them. I asked if she had thought of staying over the winter. Her answer was not at all what I expected. 'My fiancé would wonder what I was thinking.' My mind sort of stumbled, but I finally asked, 'How long have you known Sam?' Careen and Sam laughed, and then she replied, 'I've known my big brother ever since the day I was born!' The look on my face suddenly brought a serious quietness to the trio. Sam broke the silence saying that Careen was his only sister, and he had talked her into accompanying him to Nome for a few weeks. He was taking her to the Missouri Mine the next day for a tour of the operation, before she left.

"I couldn't remain standing there any longer because I felt a shortness of breath that would soon consume me. As if planned in advance, the telephone rang; I excused myself and ducked into the sewing room to answer the call. When I finished, instead of rejoining Molly and the others, I quietly climbed the stairs to the apartment. The children were playing at a friend's house, which was a relief because it would have upset them to see me so sad. I had been crushed by the thought of Sam marrying another. The fact that I cared so much, affirmed the depth of love I felt for Sam. I sincerely loved him, like no other time before. But I would have to learn how to live without him. It appeared that Sam had moved past his last words to me, since he had made no move to talk privately. I wanted so much to be loved by this man. I would be twenty-four years old in a few days and wondered just when would I love and be loved in return?"

"I knew it!" Ray cheered. "I just knew he wasn't married!"

"Oh, Ray, you are so silly!" Rosalie said. "You were as surprised as I was, and Abigail, as far as that goes."

"Grandma told me this part of her story so many times," Callie said.

Rosalie asked, "Now, did she leave Nome that summer?"

"After all the talk about going back to Oregon, Abigail came to realize she would never leave Etta behind; it was impossible to think of the children without Etta."

Rosalie pointed out, "But she leaves at some point, since they ended up back in Oregon."

"Well, yes. You've wanted me to skip ahead with parts of Abigail's life, so I'll tell you something about Faith," Callie offered.

"You've said that Faith is your mother," Ray reminded himself.

"Yes, but it gets better. Faith married Alice's youngest son, Cal. And they had me!" Callie laughed.

"Oh, I should have figured that out since you were named after him," Rosalie confessed.

Ray asked, "What happened after Abby found out Sam wasn't married after all?"

"After Sam and Careen stayed at the mine a few days, they both returned to town until she left for Colorado. Abby stayed in the apartment most days to avoid coming face to face with Sam," Callie said, as she took the memoir for a turn to read.

"I loved Careen, everybody did. She had all the good qualities of her brother, was intelligent, and completely unaware she was so beautiful. Molly and I invited Careen to join us upstairs one evening. Molly gave her a fine batiste camisole, trimmed around the neck with French lace, to take home as a gift. We all had needlework in our laps so she decided to embroidery tiny pink flowers around the hem of her camisole, while we visited over our work. Careen told us about her fiancé, and shared their wedding plans. When it was time to tuck Faith and Nicholas into bed, she asked for a hug from each of them. Careen told us that Sam and his wife had been married only a year when she died; the family thought he had lost his mind, his grief was so deep. He resigned his position at the college and finally the Klondike beckoned. Nothing could hold him back once Frank agreed to go with him.

"Careen left in mid-July on the same steamer as the Robertsons; we invited all of them for a farewell dinner the night before sailing. Frank brought Etta and Henry to town, and I knew Sam would attend our little party with his sister. We missed Robert but the Missouri Mine was taking advantage of long days and good weather, working around the clock. I had an eerie feeling all evening that someone was watching me, but I presumed it wasn't Sam since he barely looked my way. The children were so excited to see him again, and he seemed touched by their attention. Sam offered to pat Henry on the back for a burp, while Etta was busy in the kitchen. The scene was so tender I felt like my pounding heart would burst from its cage. When our friends readied to leave, Careen pulled me aside into the kitchen, and whispered, 'I don't know what happened between you and Sam, but he cares for you very much.' Stuttering, I replied, 'Oh, Careen, I don't think so anymore.' She smiled, saying, 'A sister knows.' Just before I went to my bedroom, Etta said, 'Abby, Sam couldn't take his eyes off of you tonight.' How could I have missed that?"

"My nightmare with Lars just wouldn't go away! I walked the children to the beach, to bid Careen and Ida good-bye one last time when they boarded the barge. Sam escorted Careen onboard, and then returned to shore as the tug boat pulled the barge away towards their ship anchored offshore. We stood side by side, waving at the passengers, when Sam said, 'Someone is trying to catch your eye.' I followed where he was pointing onboard the barge, and there stood Lars, who tipped his hat when he noticed I saw him. I turned around and said bitterly, 'I wish I'd never met the man.' It suddenly dawned on Sam that it was Lars, but he regained the steely look in his eyes and I couldn't tell what he was thinking. Right then, Nicholas and Faith grabbed my hands, and begged to go to the candy shop. We three walked quickly down Front Street, amid crowds of smiling men and women. I almost hated them for their cheerfulness."

X V

. . . .

"I WOKE THE NEXT MORNING WITH TWO TOUSLE headed cherubs curled next to me. What in the world was I feeling so sad about? I had let myself be defined by whether a man loved me or not, and had forgotten the blessings which surrounded me every day. My children were more precious to me than I can describe. Every morning they woke me with their hugs and kisses; how could I ask for more than that? Molly and Etta were my steadfast confidantes, whose loyalties never wavered. I couldn't be bitter about those years in the North, because if I hadn't gone, I wouldn't have known those bounties of the heart.

"Our friend, Kate, was a concern to all of us; a recent letter from Nevada sounded like she was a bit lost in the world. Kate was staying with an actress she knew from Dawson City, who ran a guest ranch near Reno. Kate said she was singing with a band for the guests' evening entertainment; yet, she didn't sound very happy.

"Frank came to town in August with an infected foot, after he had stepped on a large nail in an upturned timber. After treating it himself at the mine for two weeks, Frank saw the doctor who admitted him to the hospital. With aggressive treatment, we hoped and prayed that he wouldn't lose that foot. Etta, in her quiet way, was terrified because she knew the danger of such an infection. Each of us had known someone who'd lost a loved one to similar injuries; it was very frightening. When Frank was finally on the mend, Etta looked like a ton of rocks had been lifted off her shoulders. He did lose some flesh on the side of his right foot, which took a long time to heal, but we were just relieved he wasn't worse off.

"Sam, Robert and Frank took thousands of dollars out of the Missouri Mine that summer, enough to set each of them up in business, or to buy a big ranch. Then, out of the blue, a conglomerate of mine investors made an offer to buy the mine; the three men seemed inclined to accept the terms. I was afraid to ask Etta what she and Frank would do afterwards.

"Molly and Robert told all of us they were not going on a honeymoon that winter to travel outside. She had never really liked Nome, but they weren't ready to leave the North just yet. Molly discovered that her old building in Dawson was sitting vacant, and asked Robert if he would help move her business. Robert would have done anything for Molly, so they packed up the inventory. The three partners sold the Missouri Mine, which seemed like the right thing to do. The shop that Tom built for Molly in Nome two years earlier was sold to a haberdasher, who had just arrived from Kansas City. The situation was almost funny: Molly wouldn't have to work another day in her life, but she so loved what she did best, that it was hard for her to give it up. As fate would have it, just as I'd thought of leaving Nome for Oregon, Molly asked if I would consider working one more year with her in Dawson. To help me decide, Etta said she would like to move back to Dawson, to be closer to her sister for a time. Frank agreed, as long as it wouldn't be permanent; Etta promised him that she would leave Dawson the next year.

"I knew that Sam thought I was 'prickly' whenever we found ourselves in the same room; Etta scolded me for building a barrier against Sam getting close to me again. But I knew that no matter what he might say, down deep he would always consider me tainted by my past. I could live with it, but I would never believe he could."

"I'd have never guessed Abigail would move back to Dawson," Rosalie said.

"Grandma told me she was worried about moving back to Oregon, where society still put restrictions on women. Her adult life had been spent with a great deal of freedom, and the longer she was in the North, the more she worried about living anywhere else," Callie explained, and they continued reading.

"Getting to Dawson wasn't anything like when I traveled on the steamer to become a bride in the Klondike exactly five years ago. Steaming up the Yukon River was much more comfortable this time, and there wasn't the feeling of urgency to get to Dawson City before everybody else. However, the captain was anxious to get his steamer to Dawson before the river started to freeze up for the winter. We saw a large number of wrecked boats on the way, some burned to the waterline, along the river's edge. Any that weren't pulled far enough up the beach to bleach in the sun, were swept down river when the ice broke up in the spring. Some villages previously bustling with activity were deserted; others had just sprung up to fulfill the needs of a few miners in the area. Indians were still drying fish on racks, and selling cords of wood to the steamers. The *Thomas Jefferson* wasn't hauling much cargo; therefore, we made good time plowing against the current to our destination. This trip was easier since Faith and Nick were older, and understood the rules of staying safe on the boat. There were two other children onboard, so I believe time passed quickly for the twins. On October 10, 1903 the *Thomas Jefferson* tied up at the Dawson City dock. A few days later our boat was winched up on skids set far back from the river, ready to carry the first passengers to St. Michaels in June.

"Dawson City's population was much smaller than when we left, since large mining companies had bought almost all of the small claims and many folks had left. The center of town still had its core of shops, banks, saloons, and restaurants; however, farther out, buildings were vacant with missing window glass and weeds had taken over doorways. Maison de Mode needed a coat of paint, inside and out, but only one window pane was broken. Robert inspected the roof for loose metal sheeting or rusted out holes. Street after street had empty cabins but it seemed like the nicer homes remained occupied. There was a sense of civilized life in the slightly worn-down town. A new school had replaced the old one, and the city was in contact with the outside world by telegraph. Etta had wonderful news when we arrived: her sister Asa's husband had opened a grocery in Dawson, and they lived above the store, just a few steps from Maison de Mode!

"The cabin that Barrett built on the hill was in good condition, and there was such comfort in unbolting the door and entering the undisturbed room. I was so happy to return, and Etta grinned from ear to ear! Once the claw-foot table was back in place with the silk scarf draped over it, I felt a calmness wash over me, confirming that our return to Dawson was the right thing to do. Frank and Robert were working day and night to prepare us for winter which was close on our heels. Frank hired a man to haul firewood and water, since he and Robert started with the shop renovations. My cabin was too small for three adults and three children, so Frank, Etta and baby Henry moved into a vacant house just a stone's throw away. Molly was encouraged that her business would once again be successful, judged by the number of ladies who poked their heads in the door, excited to see her back. One of the seamstresses who worked for Molly three years ago came in to ask for a job; we all said 'Yes!' in unison. The re-opening was set for the next Saturday, and we expected to have an overwhelming amount of business.

"I wrote Kate from Nome about our sudden move back to Dawson City, and hoped a letter would be waiting for me. I was sadly disappointed, but anticipated one would arrive with each mail delivery."

January 2, 1904

Dawson City, Yukon Territory

Dear Alice,

The children and I are back in Dawson City, with friends Molly and Robert, plus Etta, Frank and baby Henry. We opened the Maison de Mode once more, and hired another seamstress. Etta comes in about half a day, and her sister, Asa, asked if she could do handwork for us in the evenings. Dawson's women are so ready for new fashions that they have swamped us with orders.

Many old acquaintances have quit the Yukon Territory, and Dawson is a shell of the town it was in the heyday of the gold rush. The folks who are left make up a more stable community, with regular city services and businesses. Electricity now extends to all parts of town, including a new line to my cabin! It's wonderful to walk into a dark room, and turn a knob to illuminate a bulb instead of fumbling with the oil lamp. My eyes are not so strained now while sewing during these dark winter evenings.

Nicholas managed to break his left arm sledding down the hill just outside our door. The doctor assures me it was a clean break, and should heal perfectly in about two months. Nick is very proud of his cast, but I'll be surprised if he doesn't break the other arm. My son is such a daredevil! Being active four-year olds, Faith and Nick were bored just hanging around the shop while I sewed or fitted dresses, so I enrolled them in Miss Jones' Academy. She teaches a half-day class of four and five year olds, mostly about manners, drawing, and singing. They come back to the shop by lunchtime, happy and tired!

While bent over our sewing, Etta and I reminisce about the winter we spent alone here after Barrett died. I remember how frightened I felt at times. She confesses that she was a bit afraid of me at first; then she was afraid I would leave the Klondike. I feel that over the last five years I have been riding wave after wave of emotions; sometimes I am on the crest, riding high with excitement, but other times I am in the trough and unable see a way out.

Mother writes that she is well and my brothers are putting more effort into their schooling, which pleases her immensely. Emily's summer with the excavation team has convinced her she made the correct choice of careers.

A small room I had built onto the cabin was the best idea I've had in a long time. The twins love their own private place, with box beds thickly insulated with furs, and room for their toys. It opens into the main room, so the stove which burns all night helps keep it warm.

I enjoyed this Christmas more than any other we've celebrated; I suppose it's because the children are older and getting interested in the traditions and gift giving. Nicholas took great pride in making Etta and Molly drawings of the steamer that brought us back to Dawson City. He is quite good! Faith helped me make batches of fudge to fill boxes for our friends. We chopped down a small spruce tree and dragged it into the cabin one very cold day to decorate with dried berry garlands and cookie ornaments.

Although Frank wouldn't have to work in Dawson City, he got so bored "hanging around the girls" that he decided to freight supplies to the road houses spread along the routes to far-flung claims. Etta is happy to have him pleased with himself, since she is the one who wanted to come back here this year. Henry is a happy baby all of the time. Faith and Nick love to push him around the shop in a box, which makes him giggle until he falls over!

Sam did not accompany us to Dawson City, and left Nome on a ship bound for Seattle before we even boarded our boat for the Yukon. He told Frank that he would stay in Colorado until after Careen's wedding in November. Frank received a note from Sam recently; he was in San Francisco and didn't mention any future plans. I don't know why I keep thinking about Sam, since he is one more closed chapter in my life.

How are your children? Please write me all the news from Shaniko! Your friend,

Abigail

"A terrible storm kept us imprisoned in the cabin for a week during February. We had ample food and fuel, and Frank came to check on us about every other day. Our usually calm days here on the flats of the Yukon River were decidedly turbulent, with winds erratically gusting day and night. It reminded me of the storms we had in Nome, with snow being picked up and driven against structures. The tiniest crack in the wall or door was soon decorated with a rim of ice and snow on the floor below it, until I sealed it with something. Faith and Nick were so bored with staying inside, not being able to visit with their friends in town, or even play with Henry.

"When the storm finally blew itself out, Molly trudged up the hill, stopped to collect Etta and Henry, and arrived at my doorstep early one morning. She handed me a copy of the Nome Nugget, and both friends watched my reaction after pointing to the front page headlines. '*Bigamist Jensen Arrested In San Francisco*'. I thrust the paper back in Molly's hands, and asked her to read it to me. According to the article, Lars' real wife Myra, who had neither divorced him nor died, found out about his marriage in Sacramento, and contacted an investigator. Once the details were known, Lars was arrested. It seems that the story he wove so intricately to explain his and Jimmy's journey to the gold fields, was to cover up that he and Myra were embroiled in a bitter custody fight for Jimmy. He thought they would never be located; however, his greed for fame and wealth was his undoing. What a terrible thing that Lars included Jimmy in his deception; I was such a fool to believe his lies. He was out on bail, but his reputation, marriage and any thoughts of a political career, were ruined. All of sudden, Etta started to giggle, and then Molly; I soon joined in, and by that time, Nick and Faith were laughing and dancing. It was a wonderful afternoon!

"The next week Frank brought another copy of the Nome Nugget to show us a small article headed *Mine Developer Collins Arrested in S.F.* The details spelled out how 'Sam Collins assaulted Lars Jensen in a hotel bar. Collins told the arresting officer that Jensen insulted a young woman in Nome, and deserved a worse punishment than he received.' The judge fined Collins for disturbing the peace, after Jensen dropped all charges.' I couldn't believe it! Etta said, 'I tried to tell you that Sam still cares about you. Now if you can soften up a little, we will get this straightened out.' I hugged her and agreed that she was right, as usual.

"That afternoon I ran down to the telegraph office, and sent a message to the hotel where Sam was staying in San Francisco. I just said, 'Sam STOP Come back STOP Abby.'

"Two long weeks elapsed before we heard from Sam, and I had almost given up hope. Etta came to the cabin and handed me a telegram which had been delivered to the shop. I ripped it open and read 'Abby STOP Returning to Dawson STOP Sam.' The telegram was sent from Skagway, so he was coming down the icy Yukon River from Whitehorse, and would arrive within two weeks. Oh, the days were long as I sat by the window and watched for a familiar form coming up the trail. Could we really salvage our love for each other?

"On March 16 Frank received a telegram from a doctor in Whitehorse. Sam had arrived at a roadhouse just northwest of Lake LeBarge two days earlier. He was so ill with a high fever and delirium that he couldn't be moved. The doctor advised that a family member should come very soon! I begged Frank to take me with him on the sled, and he agreed. I had to see Sam again. We left that very afternoon."

"Did she get there in time?" Rosalie asked. "Did Sam survive?"

Ray said, "It must have taken them several days to get to him."

"Frank thought they could make the trip in a week, but the weather just wouldn't give them a break," Callie replied. "Abby next described the trek and what happened when they arrived."

X V I

· ·

"IN MATTERS OF THE HEART, I SHOULD GET A FAIL-
ing grade. Falling in love with Sam became troublesome only because
I had developed mistrust of men in general, and of myself. It was
only when I thought all was lost, that I realized how deep my love
was for him.

"We feverishly began gathering what was needed for the trek. He
assembled a dog team of 12 malamutes to pull a sled large enough to
carry winter clothes, bedding, salmon for the dogs, and essential supplies for survival in case we had to camp between roadhouses. After
I kissed Faith and Nick good bye, Molly and Etta hugged me tight
and tried to convince me that Sam was in good hands. As we pulled
away from the shop, I couldn't look back at my children watching
out the windows; I knew they would be well cared for, but I felt torn
from their grasps.

"The weather was almost spring-like the first day out, and we
stopped at the Forks Hotel for the night. I couldn't sleep, for worrying about Sam; when Frank roused me at five o'clock, I drank several
mugs of coffee while he harnessed the team. When we stopped at
ten to rest the dogs, and heat a pot of soup, Frank confided that he
hadn't slept either. I had planned to run alongside the sled for much
of each day, but discovered that I didn't have the stamina at first.
Although the dogs had no problem pulling the sled with my added

weight, I was much colder just sitting motionless. The second day on the trail was long, and by the time we reached the next roadhouse, my feet were numb, which alarmed Frank. Thank goodness I had no damaging frostbite, but from then on he kept the dogs from sprinting down the fast trail, so I could trot with them most of the day. We were eating well since the roadhouses along the Yukon served plain but tasty food, and lots of it. When we stopped each night, the first thing we had to do was unpack frozen salmon to feed the dogs, and melt ice for their water. Every third night, Frank heated a large pot of water and added a mixture of dried meat and cornmeal to cook into a mush for our loyal team.

"The fourth night found us between roadhouses; however, the temperature was not too cold, maybe twenty below. Frank and I pitched the small tent, and covered the floor with small spruce branches to give us some insulation from the snow. Over this we spread blankets to make a mattress, so when we each rolled up into our own fur robes, the night was tolerable. The malamutes had no problems sleeping in such weather; after their feeding, they simply curled up for the night. Sometimes we had snow overnight, and awakened to find white lumps scattered around the site, whether it be outside a roadhouse or near our tent. Each dog was tied to a stake or tree to keep him from running off to join other dogs or simply to chase a rabbit. Our situation could have been deadly if we lost the team in a remote area along the river. The sled ran smoothly on the river's ice, but we still had to watch for snags frozen into the surface. I'd been able to run beside the sled more each day, and felt guilty when I had to ride for awhile. It seemed like we would never reach Sam.

"On the fifth day we met two teams headed for Dawson, and stopped to share a hot lunch and rest the dogs. The teams were part of a Canadian Royal Mounted Police patrol, searching for a missing missionary. Later we heard that he was found frozen, in an abandoned cabin near Minto. Our fifth night was spent at Fort Selkirk, a fair sized community settled long ago by traders and Canadian Police. Dinner revived our exhausted bodies, so we sat before the fireplace and talked for awhile. According to Frank, Sam didn't understand why I walked out the day I told him about Lars. If we had only been able to talk about it, I would have understood that Sam didn't want me to apologize for anything; he loved me. At that moment though, he was in shock with all I had said, and I had a chip on my shoulder. I tearfully told Frank I wish there were some way we could find out about Sam's condition while on the trail; I couldn't bear to think he might already be dead. Emotionally, I was a wreck that evening so Frank talked me into having a shot of whisky, which did its job: I slept in spite of my worries. We woke to a warning about the weather, but had to keep moving. Fort Selkirk was over half-way between Dawson and Whitehorse, and our destination was located about a day closer to us. Frank sent a telegram to the doctor, informing him of our location, and approximate day of arrival. We talked about asking for news of Sam's condition, but the answer might not come for another day, and Frank agreed that we should put more miles behind us.

"I prayed that Sam could understand we were coming as fast as possible. The skies cleared that day, but the temperature had dropped considerably by the time we pulled up to a riverside hotel in the evening. Although we hadn't met many travelers on the river, the hotel was filled with miners who were escaping from their claims in nearby creeks and canyons. There were no individual rooms, just one large floor upstairs with straw mattresses on which to spread our own robes. The only other woman besides me was the hotel owner, and she said I should sleep in her room just off the kitchen, which was a relief.

"Only one other team besides ours left early the next morning, and they were headed to Dawson. Mid-morning we met the mail sledge, and Frank asked him about the trail ahead. The mail carrier said the trail was firm, but his bones indicated a weather change was coming. He was so right! By two o'clock snow was blowing into our faces and I continually stumbled so much I finally had to get into the sled. Frank said we could not reach the next roadhouse that night, since he could hardly see the trail. The wind was so severe on the wide, exposed river that we pulled the team up into the woods to build a camp. By the time the dogs were fed, we realized putting up the tent was useless, since the wind was whipping about terribly. Frank scouted the area and found a safe place in the lee of an old uprooted tree, where we built a fire in front of the lean-to Frank and I hastily constructed. Over the fire I thawed caribou jerky from our stash, and toasted bread slices. Mugs of hot coffee washed everything down and thawed my insides. Frank gathered a huge pile of dry limbs from the upturned tree, to keep the fire fueled all night; we wrapped in our fur robes and tried to sleep. All night the wind howled and I could hear crashing in the forest, most likely from trees falling or limbs breaking off. I couldn't tell if it was still snowing or just the snow already on the ground being swirled aloft by the wind.

"Sometime during the long night, Frank gathered several dogs around us for warmth. Unaccustomed to sleeping with humans, they were uneasy with the arrangement, but I appreciated their impact on my comfort. Morning offered no change in the weather; the only safe thing to do was wait out the storm, but it tore me apart just sitting by the fire, wasting valuable time on the trail. Frank gathered more firewood while I heated water for the dogs, and then for our tea. We chewed on jerky, and Frank talked about how happy he is with Etta and Henry in his life. He saw Sam's pain when his wife died, and better understood why he was so crushed. The winds switched direction by noon, still so strong that our campfire kept blowing out. Finally, we huddled together under layers of robes, with dogs close by. It was nearly dark before the wind and snow eased, but at least we were able to sleep more comfortably.

"Frank woke me very early, and we packed the sled under a clear, starlit sky. The original trail had been swept away, so we had to strike out down the river, breaking trail for miles and miles. About nine o'clock we met a cargo sled from Lake Bennett, heading for Fort Selkirk; after that, we made better time on the broken trail. I had to run beside the sled most of the day, since two dogs had frostbitten their paws, so they had to ride. By taking one brief rest mid-day, we arrived in Carmacks about six o'clock; a real bed never looked so good! I was embarrassed at the amount I ate, but couldn't stop myself when the cook slid a platter of roasted moose, potatoes, onions, and hot bread in front of me. By the time I sponged off some of the sweat and dog smell my eyes couldn't stay open any longer.

"Our last day on the trail began early, under a cloudless sky. We left the two lame dogs in Carmacks, so I could ride in the sled and make faster time. Frank must have talked to the dogs about what was expected that day, for they flew up the trail like the sled was on fire! I trembled with excitement and dread at the same time, anticipating the moment I would arrive at Sam's side. Would he be alright, or would I be too late? When we finally pulled up in front of the roadhouse that night, the rooms downstairs were brightly lit, but only one light shined through a window upstairs, and I knew that was Sam's room. By the time the dogs were secured, their barking had announced our arrival and a raw-boned woman stepped out on the porch. She looked at my face, and asked, 'Are you Abby?' When I nodded, she just pointed upstairs, and I ran, pounding up the carpeted steps, discarding parka, scarves, gloves, and hat as I went.

"As I approached the landing, Sam stepped from his room, steadying himself against the wall. In an instant I was in his arms, and we kissed as if for the first time. He finally brought his hands up to cradle my face, and with his lips a bare inch from mine, he murmured, 'I love you, Abby. I can't live without you.' Sam crushed me to him as we kissed again, and then it was my turn to say, 'I will never leave your side, my love.'

"I realized that Sam was very weak, and led him to the bed where we sat together. He took my hands, looked into my eyes and said, 'That day when we stood together on the beach when Careen left, I wanted to take you in my arms. You seemed so distant and hard, that I lost hope. I was a fool for not begging you right then to give us a chance.'

"I tearfully told him that I was so afraid of being hurt again; I convinced myself that if I were the one who walked away, it would be easier. I was so wrong.

"Sam smiled a little as he told me about his confrontation with Lars. He and a friend met for drinks at a hotel in San Francisco. Sam said 'I could hear a conversation at the next table, a man mostly boasting of his conquests with money and women. He said only one woman had got under his skin, but he had married another. When I looked over my shoulder, I saw Lars bragging about his proposition to have the young mother as his mistress…' I stopped Sam then, saying that I knew the ending of the story, and he said, 'I do too, now. It was very satisfying seeing Lars spread out on the floor.' Tears fell between us as we embraced, and I could tell he was tired from the exertion of the last few minutes. I tucked Sam into bed, and told him we would talk more in the morning, but I would stay in his room all night. Frank had been hanging back in the doorway, and went to Sam's side before he slept. The cousins clasped arms, and Sam said, 'You brought her through quite a storm, I hear.' Frank replied, 'Like I had a choice!'

"It was two weeks before Sam was strong enough to make the trip back to Dawson City; however Frank missed Etta and Henry terribly and left after two days at Lake LeBarge. He arranged our transport with a freighting outfit; after an easy trip we arrived back at my cabin on May 5. Oh, I scooped the children into my arms and hugged them until they complained! During my time with Sam, both at Lake LeBarge and on the trail home, we talked out all our miscommunication, preconceived notions, and prideful hesitation. How we could have been so attracted to each other, and not cleared up the mistakes earlier, was absurd. But I believe that our love, especially a hard-won love, was sweeter for it. I told Sam all about my life before we met, and he did the same. He just said we would have fabulous stories to tell our grandchildren about our years in the Klondike and Nome, but we would make our own history to write from that time forward.

"That spring when I said I was returning to Oregon, it was true. Sam asked me to marry him before our steamer took us up the Yukon River, to rendezvous with a ship in Skagway bound for Seattle. Etta and Frank had yet to decide where they would be the next year; however, I knew she would convince him Oregon had room for us all. Molly and Robert wanted to stay in the North at least another year, since he wanted to prospect in a valley up the Pelly River. Molly sold the millinery business to one of her dedicated seamstresses (for very little money, I would bet), and accompanied Robert on his quest. I wrote to Kate at her last known address, to let her know where to find me by summer's end. I wanted so much to hear she was alright.

"I left the Klondike with a light heart, and pieces of so many people in my mind. All of them had a hand in shaping who I had become over those six years, so I honestly had no regrets. Well, maybe one or two!"

"That's Grandma Abigail's last entry in her memoir," Callie softly said. Rosalie slumped back in her chair, not realizing until then she had been leaning forward to catch every word about Abigail's dash to Sam's side. Ray let out a sigh, and then laughed at himself for it.

"Surely you are going to tell us what happened later," Rosalie said.

"You've come this far with her, I figured you'd want to know," Callie said.

Rosalie hesitated before saying, "Maybe I shouldn't mention this, but after I read that Abby had the twins, you took the journal next, and it appeared you skipped a page ahead when you began reading. Am I wrong?"

Callie answered directly, "No, you aren't wrong. I wasn't sure I wanted you to know about my grandma's secret…I think it's ok now. A few days after Faith and Nick were born, Abby wrote an honest admission of those circumstances, which was never spoken of again. Only Etta and her sister Asa, Molly and Kate knew, until Abby told Sam and many years later when she dictated this memoir to me."

"If you'd rather not, we'd understand," Ray said. "After all, I already feel privileged to have learned about your grandmother and the Klondike on such a personal level." Rosalie nodded, with a serious expression on her face.

"That's sweet of you, but allow me to complete Abigail's story. It will explain a lot of her decisions," Callie replied. She flipped back through the memoir, and found what Abby wrote about the babies' births.

"The calendar on the wall indicated it was June 8, 1899 and I had two babies with milky drool slipping from their lips, asleep in a box by my bed. Sweet little Faith had downy red hair and fair skin, and Nicholas reminded me of my youngest brother as a newborn. Faith was Etta's baby, fathered by Barrett. If this had been known publically, most people would've insisted that I banish Etta from my home; however, I placed the blame entirely on Barrett. He took advantage of an inexperienced young girl which was unforgiveable in my eyes. Barrett was no better than hundreds of other white men in the North who used those girls, then left them behind when it was time to return to their wives and fiancés. When Etta and her sister saw that Faith resembled her father so much, they knew everyone would know the truth. Neither Etta nor Faith would've had a fair life going forward from this scandal. I adored Etta for trusting me enough to bring her baby daughter to me right away. Since only Etta's sister and my friends Molly and Kate knew Faith's true parenthood, we concocted the story that Etta's baby died, and Faith and Nick were my twins. I could never separate her from her own daughter, so at her suggestion, Etta became the babies' devoted nanny. I understood then that Barrett's indiscretions (there were other rumors) were what alienated him from the church, but I would see to it that none of this ever affected the children. As soon as I became fit, I registered their births naming me and Barrett as the parents, to make certain everything was legal. Etta told me that from that time forward, she would not refer to Faith as anything but 'Abby's baby girl.' I knew it killed her inside to relinquish her first born; I insisted that she continue to nurse Faith, but I never saw a hint of favoritism as the children grew up.

"Some might ask how I could be so willing to accept Faith as my own child and hide the truth. After all, I would be leaving the Klondike behind someday. If months were counted, I too had something to hide. While Faith was Barrett's daughter, Nicholas was not his son. Again, only my close friends knew this. I didn't take the children into town for several weeks, so the age differences wouldn't be so obvious. Although I had been tempted a time or two, to tell Lars about Nick, I was so thankful I did not. Those children were mine and Barrett's.

"I am totally blown away; never saw it coming!" Ray exclaimed.

"Me neither!" Rosalie added. "I guess I just assumed the twins arrived a bit premature. Gosh, I'm having a hard time wrapping my head around all this."

A tap on the door, followed by a curly, salt and pepper head of hair got everyone's attention.

"Hi, Mom, I finally made it! Oh, you must be Mr. and Mrs. Evans; I'm so glad you're still here. I'm Careen." Callie's daughter was about Rosalie's age, and taller than her mother had probably been as a younger woman.

The mother and daughter embraced; although Callie said her daughter was citified, they seemed very close. Rosalie noticed the affection Careen showed her mother.

"Callie has been gracious in sharing your family history with us," said Rosalie. Ray added, "And we know you were named after your... let's see... great-great-aunt, right?"

"Oh, you've been paying attention!" Careen laughed.

Callie said, "I was just about to tell them about your Great-Grandma Abby's move back to Oregon."

"Mom and I have read the letters written to Alice, over and over," Careen said, and turning to Callie, "While you tell the rest of the family story, I'm going to change into my sweats. Have you thought about supper?"

Callie answered, "Why don't you call the pizza place and have a large one delivered?" And to Rosalie and Ray, she asked, "I'm assuming that you like pizza. Am I right? "

Ray responded, "Our favorite take out choice, and I'm buying!"

As she walked down the hall, Careen thought to herself that Callie seemed happier today than any time since Lem died. All this recollecting of family history had obviously boosted her Mom's spirits.

XVII

. . . .

"WHEN GRANDMA ABBY AND ETTA WERE IN THE LAST few years of their lives, they would reminisce for hours about the early years, and what happened just after they came to Oregon," Callie began. "I had already heard most of the stories, but if I played like a fly on the wall, and not say a word, occasionally they would reveal something new."

"Grandma Abby was the happiest she'd ever been in her life, as Sam's wife on that voyage to Seattle. Their wedding became a community event attended by dozens of sourdoughs and cheechakoes alike. The ceremony was private, in the judge's office; however, the reception had to be held in Dawson City's waterfront park. Food filled several tables, and a band played until midnight. After tucking the children into bed, Sam and Abby sat on the bench outside her cabin, watching the Klondike sun linger in a sky filled with pink and purple streaked clouds. Having waited so long to reach this point of their love, Sam was inclined to carry Abby off to their bedroom right away. However, experience held him back, knowing they would live on the memory of this night for many years, so they kissed in the dusk, murmured promises of love, and slowly undressed when finally inside their room. All of Abigail's heartaches and doubts melted away forever.

"Just a few days later, the whole family boarded a steamer for Lake LeBarge, on the first leg of their voyage home. Her children were healthy and excited, and the family in Oregon knew they were finally coming home.

"Cities and types of transportation had changed so very much in the last six years; for awhile Abby thought she had made a huge mistake by keeping Faith and Nick so isolated in the North. Later she was pleased when one or the other would recall a particular adventure or custom from those early years. I remember Mother speaking of the immense Yukon River and watching the ice jams; she said the long summer days were Nick's favorite time in the Klondike summers, when kids never wanted to go to bed! As the children grew up, Grandma Abby felt they were more accepting of different types of people, possibly from living close to the poor, Indians and Eskimos, and broken spirits. I know my Mother always tried to make the world around her fair for everyone.

"Abigail's homecoming in Prineville revolved around the immediate family, like she wanted. The railroad had built a spur to Shaniko, and they took the stage from there. Abby had decided to not tell Alice of her return, until she had time to see her mother first. She told her children how nervous she had been on that first trip away from home, but Sam told them instead that they had a very brave mommy. Abby's mother and Mr. Carter met the stage in a pouring rain, bustled them all into the hotel to wait out the storm. The two women could not stop hugging and crying; suddenly two tall young men dashed into the hotel and lifted Abby off her feet, swinging her around and around. She couldn't believe how grown up her little brothers were! All this time, Faith and Nick stood quietly to the side, wide-eyed, holding Sam's hands. Their grandmother knelt beside them, and asked if they knew who she was; Faith spoke first, saying, 'Grandma May.' Everyone loved Sam, and Abby could see that Mr. Carter made her mother very happy. Emily and her fiancé arrived the next day: a statuesque young lady on the arm of a tanned, bespectacled man. The couple married a year later, and became well-known in their field of archaeology.

"A few days after their arrival in Prineville, Sam, Abby and the children drove back to Shaniko to visit the Storey ranch. Alice chided her for not stopping on their way through, but it was a wonderful reunion between the two women. From that time on, Alice's children, William, Cal and Louise, were forever linked to Abby's family. Faith grew into a raving beauty, with translucent skin and wavy red hair; Cal, my father, was smitten at first sight, and they married in 1922, settling down on a ranch near Antelope. Cal's brother Bill took over the Story ranch, which I inherited in 1972.

"Sam and Abigail had spent long hours discussing what they would do, and where they would live, once back in the states. They agreed that locating close to family was important for Faith and Nick, so they agreed to live in Oregon, and visited Colorado often. Sam's gold mine fortune enabled them to buy a large spread on the Crooked River near Paulina, about fifty miles from Prineville. They had a little girl in 1908, my Aunt May, who was quite a horsewoman and later married a Pendleton doctor. Sam and Abby generously supported many central Oregon charities, and Sam was a driving force behind the county school district. Sadly, Nick died in France during World War I, and Sam was tragically killed when thrown from his horse in 1938. After that, Abby decided to sell the ranch, and for a few years she travelled quite a lot. Emily and Walter always welcomed Abby at their excavation sites in Egypt, claiming she was their best pottery sorter. I think she also loved interacting with the different people in faraway lands.

"Growing up on the ranch in Antelope, I had the run of thousands of acres, and I think I inherited my dad's love of the land. When Lem and I returned to Oregon after the war, Grandma Abby and Aunty Etta gave us the money to buy our own ranch near Prineville. We had wonderful family reunions, picnics, and holidays which involved the expanding clan. You know, when you get my age, it's customary to wonder if what we've done made a difference in the world. I don't know the answer to that, but I do know Lem and I were happy; losing our son in Vietnam was the only thing that kept our lives from being perfect. I'm certain that Grandma Abby and Sam felt the same way when Nick died."

Rosalie felt an emotional tug towards the old woman, knowing that retelling the latter part of her life brought an element of sadness to the moment.

"Hey, what happened to Etta and Kate? You left them out of the end of your story," Ray pointed out.

"Oh, I hadn't forgotten about them!" Callie laughed.

Just then, Careen stepped back into the room, and announced that the pizza was on its way. "So, what do you think about Abigail's adventure in the Klondike?"

"I've never heard anything like it; but your mother is about to tell us what happened to Etta and Kate," Rosalie explained. Careen smiled and nodded; she knew these tales by heart.

"Frank and Etta followed the family to Oregon after a few months, and settled in Bend. It was just a tiny stage stop at that time, but Frank could see the potential for a real city springing out of the muddy streets and rough planked buildings. He was right about that, as you know. Etta became a beloved city matriarch, with a lifetime of propelling seemingly lost causes into success stories. She bravely chose not to hide her Indian heritage and was an inspiration for children attending school on the Warm Springs Reservation. For fifty years Etta and Frank never missed a graduation ceremony there or in Bend. Their son Henry became an engineer, and built many of the bridges and roads across Oregon. In the 1950's Henry was in the U.S. Congress, working tirelessly to make life better for minorities. In some circles, his work was considered the springboard for Presidents Kennedy and Johnson's Civil Rights legislation. Etta and Frank also had a daughter named Sarah, after their move to Oregon. She studied acting in New York, and had a long career on Broadway; Etta was always so proud of both her children.

"Abigail and Etta remained devoted to each other until their deaths. Not one person ever heard either woman say a negative word about the other; they each championed the other's causes. After Sam died, Abby made her home with my folks when she wasn't travelling. About twice a month, Mom drove Grandma Abby and I to Bend to join Etta for an afternoon of cooking or sewing, and I treasured those visits. Listening to their stories of the old days was the best history lesson I had. Later, I was the one who drove all of us, including my Careen, to Aunty Etta's. Grandma Abby passed away in 1960 and Etta followed her six months later. Grandmother Alice died years earlier, so I didn't have so much time with her. Alice was very quiet and re-served, but she instilled a love of reading in me that has lasted all my life. Faith passed away in 1988; I was lucky to have those remarkable women surrounding me."

"I'm so relieved that Etta stayed close to Abigail," Rosalie said.

Careen added, "I was about twelve years old when Grandma Abby and Aunty Etta died. I always thought of them as sisters, instead of friends who met in the Klondike. I remember that some of the family tried to persuade them to write a book about their part in the gold rush. They'd always say, "We were only two in the many thousands up there."

"Are they buried here, or in Bend?" Ray asked.

Careen said, "They had it all arranged, wouldn't you know. A

Collins Family plot was purchased in the Bend Cemetery, so they lay side by side, just as in life."

Rosalie suddenly teared up, and Ray handed her his handkerchief. She said, "Not everyone is so lucky to have such a loyal friend for her whole life."

Ray forced them to move on by asking, "What about Kate? Did they know where she was all this time?"

"And what happened to Molly?" Rosalie asked.

Callie said, "Molly and Robert stayed in the Klondike two more years, and made another modest gold strike southeast of Dawson City. They moved back to his farm in Missouri, and lived into their 90's. Grandma Abby got a letter from Kate about a year after they settled near Paulina, saying she was in Fairbanks, Alaska. Abby and Etta kept up with her as she traveled from Alaska to Hollywood to Washington State. Kate married and divorced, and then in 1912 she showed up in Bend, with the idea she was going to homestead. The government had just opened thousands of square miles of arid Oregon land, and she filed on some land near Brothers, just east of Bend. Nobody knows how, but she proved up on that scrubby piece of the high desert. Personally, I think Frank and Sam helped get her started with the required cabin, and other improvements. Kate married a man she knew from Klondike days, and they sold out and moved away. Some said he went back to the Klondike; at any rate, Kate came back to Bend and bought a little cottage a few doors down from the fire department. She became a one-woman auxiliary; after every fire call, she'd meet the firemen with cookies or donuts and plenty of hot coffee. Most of the town regarded Kate as an eccentric sideshow, since she always wore her Dawson costumes and old formal dresses around town. During the Great Depression, Kate made huge kettles of soup in her own kitchen to feed destitute families. Etta and Abby always kept an eye on Kate to be sure she took care of herself. No one actually knew what she had to live on, but there was talk that she sued Alex Pantages for breach of promise years after the fact, breaking their engagement as he did, and won several thousand dollars. Before I was old enough to really remember her, Kate married one more time, and moved to Cottage Grove, across the mountains. She died in the '50's, a woman who had crowded several lifetimes into those eighty years.

Callie sat back, and with a big sigh, smiled as if she was very pleased with herself. When the doorbell rang, they all jumped and laughed. While Ray took care of the pizza delivery man, Rosalie and Careen helped gather the letters into a box, and Callie collected plates, napkins, and wine glasses from the kitchen. Rosalie carried the box into the kitchen and Callie directed her to set it on the table in her breakfast nook. The oak table was old, and had some familiar features.

"Is this the same claw-foot table Abigail had in her cabin?" Rosalie asked Callie.

"Yes. We were very fortunate she thought to bring it with her. When she sold the ranch, Mother put it in the room Grandma Abby used when she stayed at our place."

"So Callie, you ranched all your life, except during World War II?" Rosalie asked.

Careen spoke first, "Did she tell you she was the first woman veterinarian in these parts?"

"No kidding!" Ray said as he set the pizza on the coffee table. Careen handed him a bottle of wine and opener.

Callie was prodded into talking about herself as they all dove into the pizza, "There was a real need for veterinarians in central Oregon, and I'd always had a way with farm animals. While Lem was overseas, I decided to tackle the studies at Washington State University. I loved it, but always kept my practice small."

"Mom just retired ten years ago; we thought she'd never stop working. But she was an awesome animal doctor!" Careen bragged.

"I think our whole family is pretty awesome, including you," Callie said with a smile.

"Speaking of family, Mom, I just found some pretty interesting information. Matt's sister got me interested in doing a DNA analysis of myself, to find out where our long ago ancestors originated, like Europe, Africa, and so on. Well, guess what? We have Native American blood in our veins!" Careen exclaimed proudly.

Good old Ray chimed in, saying, "That's really interesting! I'm adopted and don't know anything about my roots. How does that DNA testing work?"

While Careen explained the process, the four pizza lovers washed the meal down with wine, and skipped the ice cream dessert.

Ray and Rosalie said they had a big day planned on Monday, playing tourists in Bend, and thanked Callie for such a wonderful time. She walked with them to the car, each one promising to keep in touch.

Callie looked back at the house, then at the couple. "I think Careen is ready to hear the rest of Abigail's story," she said, and Rosalie smiled and nodded.

As they pulled away from the curb, Rosalie looked back to see Callie silhouetted against an orange sun, low on the horizon…like a Klondike sky.

THE END